THE DOPED DRINK

When Lew Sherry awoke he knew that he had been drugged and then carried to another place. His eyes still half open, half shut, he heard the crash of a revolver and dimly saw the red spitting of fire. Aroused fully and quickly now, Sherry started to his feet and stumbled upon a revolver lying on the floor before him. It was his own revolver!

Sherry then saw a man lying on his side, with a crimson trickle of blood down his face, and an ugly, purple rimmed blotch on his forehead. He was dead.

Suddenly, a hand struck at the door. "What the dickens is going on in there?" asked a rough voice. Finding himself in a tight corner, Sherry knew he had to escape and prepared himself—Colt in hand.

Then, no fewer than five men suddenly charged through the doorway. "Stick up your hands!" came the grim order.

MAX BRAND

THE STRANGER

WARNER BOOKS

A Warner Communications Company

The characters, places, incidents and situations in this book are imaginary and have no relation to any person, place or actual happening

CHAPTER ONE

THEY WERE holding beef out of Clayrock, for the UX outfit. Eighteen hundred steers, strong with good feeding and apt to want their own way, were quite enough for two punchers to handle, even two like Pete Lang and Lew Sherry, whose range name was "Tiny Lew." But the beef had had their fill of good grass on this day, and had been drifted enough miles to make them at once contented and sleepy. They began to lie down, slumping heavily to their knees, and so gradually down —unlike the grace of a mustang dropping for the night.

"Trouble and beef—that's all you get out of a bunch like this," said Tiny Lew, as he circled his horse quietly around the herd. "And *we* don't get the beef," he concluded.

"Shut up and start singing," said Pete Lang. "Which if you was an orator, these shorthorns wouldn't vote for you, anyway. Sing, darn you!" said Pete Lang.

"You start it, then. I got no singing in my throat tonight."

Lang began, to the tune of "My Bonnie Lies Over the Ocean":

"Last night as I lay on the prairie,
　　And looked at the stars in the sky,
I wondered if ever a cowby
　　Would drift to that sweet by and by.

"Roll on, roll on;
Roll on, little dogies, roll on, roll on;

Roll on, roll on,
Roll on, little dogies, roll on!"

"Will you quit it?" asked Tiny Lew plaintively. "It makes me ache to hear such mournful lingo."

"You've got too much education," said Lang. "I always told you so. If there was any nacheral sense born into you, it was read out in books. But there's that speckled steer got up again. Will you sing him down, sucker, or are you gunna start wrangling until the whole herd begins to mill?"

Tiny Lew tipped back his head and his bass voice flowed in a thick, rich current, carefully subdued:

"There's old 'Aunt' Jess, that hard old cuss,
    Who never would repent;
He never missed a single meal
    Nor never paid a cent.
But old Aunt Jess like all the rest
    To death he did resign
And in his bloom went up the flume
    In the days of Forty-nine."

The speckled steer lay down again with a grunt and a puff.

"A fine, soothin' song is that," sneered Pete Lang. "Let 'em have some more! You oughta be singing in a hall, Tiny."

Tiny Lew, unabashed, continued his song with another stanza:

"There is 'Ragshag' Jim, the roaring man,
    Who could outroar a buffalo, you bet;
He roared all day and he roared all night,
    And I guess he is roaring yet.
One night Jim fell in a prospect hole—
    It was a roaring bad design—
And in that hole Jim roared out his soul,
    In the days of Forty-nine."

6

"I've had enough," said Pete Lang. "Whistle to 'em, son."

Slowly, the two punchers walked or jogged their horses around the night herd, sometimes with low, soft whistles; sometimes they sang a word or two of a song and hummed the rest of it, and the great, fat steers, plump for shipping on the next day, quieted under the soothing of the familiar sounds, and with that human reassurance about them—like a wall to shut away danger of wolf or mountain lion, danger of the very stars and winds—they went to sleep.

Then the two punchers drew their horses together and let the mustangs touch noses.

"It's quite a town, Clayrock, by the look of the lights," said Tiny Lew.

"I've had my share of talking juice in yonder, under them lights," remarked Pete Lang. "It's got one trouble. The kind of red-eye they peddle there over the bar ain't made for boys, but for growed-up men. You'd better keep away from that joint, Tiny."

Tiny Lew stretched forth a hand and took his companion firmly by the back of his coat collar. Then he heaved Pete Lang a yard out of the saddle and held him dangling against the stars.

"Do I let you drop, you little, sawed-off son of a gun?" asked Tiny pleasantly.

"I'll have your gizzard out for this!" declared Pete Lang, keeping his voice equally low, for fear of disturbing the steers.

Tiny deposited him back in the saddle.

"It's so long since I've had a drink," said Tiny, "that I'm all rusty inside. I'm lined with red rust, two inches deep. I'm more full of sand than a desert. A couple of buckets full of red-eye would hardly be heard to splash inside of me, Pete."

At this, Pete Lang chuckled.

"Look here," said he. "You go in and tip over a couple. These here dogies are plumb sleepy, and I can

7

hold 'em till morning. Go in and tip over a couple, and then come back and I'll make a visit for myself, before morning."

The big man glanced over the herd. Every steer was down. Now and again, the sound of a horn clicked faintly against a horn, or a tail swished could be heard distinctly, so still was the night!

"I'd better stay," said Tiny Lew, with indecision.

"You drift, son," replied his companion. "Besides, you're only a nuisance, tonight. The thoughts that you got in your head, they'd disturb the peace of a whole town, let alone a night herd like this. Get out of here, Tiny. You've near strangled me already." He touched his throat, where the strain of his collar had chafed the skin when Sherry had lifted him from the saddle. The big fellow slapped Lang on the shoulder.

"So long, Pete. Wish me luck, and no fights, and a safe return."

"All right," said Lang, "but I warn you that a mule makes a safer ride than a hoss into Clayrock—there's so many quicksands and holes in the ground. Don't find no friends, and don't stay to make none, but just tip down a couple and come on back."

"Right as can be," said Tiny Lew, and turned his pony's nose toward the lights of town.

He rode a pinto, only fifteen hands high, but made to carry weight, even weight such as that of Tiny, and tough as a mountain goat. They split straight across country, jumping two fences that barred the way, and so entered at last the first street of Clayrock. It was a big, rambling town, with comfortable yards around the houses, and as Tiny Lew rode in, he could hear the soft rushing sound made by sprinklers on the lawns; he could smell the fragrance of the gardens, too, and the umbrella trees stood in shapely files on either side of the way.

"Civilized," said Tiny to himself. "Pete was stringing me along a little."

He came to a bridge over a little river and, in spite

8

of his hurry, he reined in his horse to watch the flash and swing of the current as it dipped around a bend in the stream. There was sufficient distance from the arched center of the bridge to the nearest houses to enable him to look about him, over the head of Clayrock, as it were; and he saw that the town was snuggled down among the hills—easy hills for riding, he judged, by the round outlines of the heads of the hills. Only to the south there was a streak of darkness against the higher sky, and the glimmer of a number of lights which he thought, at first, must be great stars.

But then he realized that stars cannot shine through such a dark cloud, and finally he was aware that it was a flat-faced cliff that rose over Clayrock—the very features of which gave the town its name, of course! The select center of the town, no doubt.

Tiny Lew went on. He had no desire to see select centers, but presently, on the farther side of the river, he found the houses closer together. The gardens ended. People were in the streets. He passed a moving-picture house where the sign was illuminated with crimson lights. And so he reached the Parker Place.

There were two larger hotels in Clayrock, but they were not like the Parker Place. It stood off a bit by itself, on a hummock, so that it was able to surround itself with a narrow wedge of lawn or garden, and it had a beaming look of hospitality. Tiny Lew Sherry did not wait for a second thought, but turned in the head of his mount toward the stable. There he saw his horse placed at a well-filled rack, and went into the hostelry.

No sooner did he push open the door than he heard a chorus sung in loud, cheerful voices—the chorus of a range song, which made him feel at home at once. He went into the bar. A dozen punchers reached out hands for him, but Sherry broke their grips and went on into the gaming room. He knew that he was too sober to drink with fellows such as these.

In the rear room there was not a great deal of light except for three bright pools of it over the three tables

9

which were occupied; but there was comparative quiet.
That is to say, the roar from the bar was like the noise
of a sea breaking on a hollow beach. It was so loud
that the bartender had to ask twice what he would have.

Sherry had no chance to answer for himself. From the
next table rose a slender form—a tall and graceful
man who tapped the bartender's shoulder.

"Not the regular poison, but some of mine," said he.
"I can see that you've made a voyage and have just
come to port, partner. And a good thirst like that
shouldn't be thrown away on the filth they have behind
the bar, out yonder."

Sherry was willing to agree. He thanked the stranger
and asked him to sit down; as a matter of fact, he already was seating himself, uninvited.

The drinks were brought. The stranger raised his
glass, and Sherry saw that the lean, brown hand of
the other shook a little.

"Drink deep!" said he.

And Sherry drank, but his mind was troubled.

CHAPTER TWO

HE WAS troubled for several reasons, any of which
would have been good enough, but the main one was
a sort of savage keenness in the eye of the other. He
was a lank man, with a yellowish skin, and a proud,
restless way of turning his head from side to side; and
in this head there was the most active and blazing pair
of eyes that Sherry ever had seen.

"You hail from where, stranger?" asked this fellow.

"I've been punching cows for the UX outfit," said Sherry. "What's your line?"

"You punch cows?" said the other, dwelling on this answer before he made his own reply. "I've seen my storms, but I've never had to duck into such a rotten port as that to weather them. Cow-punching!"

He laughed shortly, and the gorge of Sherry rose. But, like most big men, it took a long time to warm him thoroughly with anger. He was willing to waive the peculiarities of a stranger, particularly since he was drinking this man's liquor.

"You've never been a sailor?" the host asked.

"No," said Sherry.

"You've never lived, then," said the other.

"What's your name?" said Sherry.

"My name is Harry Capper. What's yours?"

"Sherry is my name. I'll let you into the know. Some of the boys around here would take it pretty hard if they heard you at work slamming punching as a trade."

"Would they? Would they?" snapped Capper, his buried eyes blazing more brightly than ever.

"You have to do the things you find to do," said Sherry with good humor. "Besides, you couldn't sail a ship through this sort of dry land."

He laughed a little at his own remarks, but Capper refused to be softened.

"I thought that you looked like a man who would be doing a man's work. There's no work off the sea. There's no life off the sea—except on an island!"

He laughed in turn, with a sort of drawling sneer. Sherry made up his mind that the wits of Harry Capper were more than a little unsettled.

"I'll tell you what I'll do," said Capper, "I'll spot any landsman ten years, and show him more life in half the time at sea. Rough and smooth. Into the wind and with it! What does a landsman ever get a chance to do? But suppose you have four thousand tons of steel under you, and the steel loaded with a cargo, and the engines crashing and smashing, and a rotten crew to work the craft, and leagues between you and your port, and a fortune if you get to it—well, that's living!"

"You've commanded a ship?"

"I never sailed in command, but I've been first officer to bring more than one ship home. You don't always finish where you start. That's one thing about the sea, too!"

Again he laughed, and more than ever Sherry was convinced that this man's brain was addled. He would have liked, too, to hear something about the steps by which the other had risen to the command of vessels when he sailed in subordinate roles. He had no opportunity, for suddenly Capper started to his feet.

He sat down again, almost at once. His nostrils quivered, and his eyes flared more villainously than ever; he was staring at Sherry with an almost murderous intensity as he said: "I'll show you some of the things that you learn at sea. Look at the fellow just coming into the room. He looks like a swell, don't he?"

Sherry saw a man of middle age come into the room and stand for a moment near the door, drawing off his gloves slowly. He had a fine, thoughtful face, a most magnificent forehead, and the whole bearing of a quiet gentleman who lives more inside himself than in the world.

"You'd say that a fine gentleman like that wouldn't talk to a bird like Harry Capper, beachcomber and what not?"

"And will he?" asked Sherry, beginning to feel a good deal of disgust.

"*I* think he will—if I ask him," said Capper. "You'll see now."

He turned suddenly in his chair.

"Hello," said he. "Come over and have a drink with me."

The newcomer started a little at the sound of this voice, but now he replied courteously: "I'm not drinking, Capper. Thank you."

12

The sailor laughed in his unusually disagreeable manner.

"You'd better think again!" he said with a great deal of ugly point.

The other hesitated for a moment; then he came to the table and sat down.

"This here is by name of Sherry," said Capper. "And this is Oliver Wilton, an old messmate of mine. Ain't you Oliver?"

The other made a little gesture which might have expressed assent, or simple irritation.

"Sure, he's a messmate of mine," said Capper. "We've sailed around the world together. We got a lot of the same charts in our heads. We've seen places. We've seen Bougainville Island, and Choiseul. And Treasury Island, and Tonongo, and Buena Vista, and San Cristoval. Have we seen them, mate?"

He reached across and slapped the shoulder of Oliver Wilton, and the latter winced from the touch of the sailor. He had refused whiskey and was merely making a pretense of sipping his beer, while he watched Capper with an extraordinary expression which, Sherry thought, contained elements of disgust, fear, and keen anger.

And the surprise of Sherry grew. It was beyond words amazing that a gentleman should submit to such familiarity from such a fellow as Capper.

"But Oliver left the sea," said Capper. "You don't mind if I call you Oliver, do you, Oliver?"

"I suppose not," said the other.

Capper grinned with delight at the torment he was inflicting.

"Of course, you don't mind," said he. "Not a good fellow and a rare sport like you—why, the things that we got to remember together would fill a book, and a good fat book, at that! Am I right, old man?"

Oliver Wilton bit his lip.

"Closed-mouth old boy he is," said Capper, "but always willing to stand his round of drinks. Slow in

13

the talk, but fast in the drinking was always his way."

At this broad hint, Wilton presently ordered a round of drinks, and Sherry could not help noticing the curious glance which the waiter cast at the sailor and at Wilton who would sit at such a table.

"You're not taking more than you can hold?" said Wilton to the sailor.

"Me?" chuckled Capper. "I always got room in my hold for the right kind of goods to be stowed away in an extra corner. Always! So bring on the new shipment!"

The drinks were duly ordered, and then Wilton said suddenly: "I'll see that they fill out of the right bottle. They have a way of substituting in this place!"

He got up and hurried from the table.

Capper leaned back in his chair, his face filled with malicious satisfaction.

'He's a rum old boy, eh?" said he. "But he's on the hook. Oh, he can wriggle if he wants to, but he can't get off the hook! It's stuck into his gills! I suppose," he went on, his face flushing with a sort of angry triumph, "that there's nothing that he wouldn't give me, if I asked for it. I start with asking for a drink, but I might ask more. Oh, I might ask a whole cargo from him. But he's got that good a heart that he never could turn down an old shipmate!"

He laughed again in that peculiarly disagreeable manner of his, and Sherry stirred in his chair. He had had enough of this company and he determined to leave after the present round. Moreover, Pete Lang would be expecting his return before long.

Wilton came back, himself carrying the tray.

"There you are," said Capper. "I told you he was a rare old sport. Pay for the drinks and play waiter to bring 'em, too. That's his way. Big-hearted and an open hand for all. That's him, always."

Wilton set down the drinks.

He seemed much more cheerful, now; though Sherry

could not help suspecting that there was something assumed in the present good nature.

But he sat down and offered the glasses with a smile.

"Good luck and good health to you, Capper," said he, "and to you!"

"Why," said Capper, leaning a little over the table, "that's a kind thing, sir. A mighty kind way of putting things. And here's to you, with all my heart!"

It seemed that Capper was genuinely moved by the cheerful manner of the man he had been tormenting, and he showed his emotion in his voice.

Sherry, in the meantime, with a nod to the others, picked up a glass, in haste to be done and away.

Half the contents were down his throat before he heard the exclamation of Wilton: "Hello! That's not your glass!"

At last, he lowered the glass. It had had rather a bitter taste, he thought. Capper, in the meantime, had finished the glass he had taken up, and hearing the alarmed exclamation of Wilton, he now snatched the one from the hand of Sherry and swallowed off the contents, saying, with his brutal laugh, "I've got to have my own, of course!"

Sherry, half disgusted, stared at Capper. His temper had been frayed thin by the repeated insolence of the other, and now the striking muscles up and down his arm began to tighten.

"I ain't had enough drinks," said Capper suddenly, "to make me feel so dizzy. I—"

He half rose from his chair and slumped heavily back into it, his head canting over upon one shoulder.

"Gents," said Sherry, "I've gotta leave you. I'll pay for a round, but then I have to start back—"

He rose in turn, and then a stunning darkness struck him back into his chair and he heard a voice, apparently from a great distance, saying: "Here is a pair of helpless drunks. What will you do with them?"

CHAPTER THREE

FLASHES OF sense returned to Sherry, thereafter. He knew that he was being dragged, half carried, to another place. He knew that he was allowed to slump heavily to the floor. And after that, he had a sense of cold and darkness. When he was able to get to his knees, his eyes were still half open, half shut, and it was at this time that he heard the crash of a revolver, inhaled the pungent fumes of burned powder, and was dimly aware of the red spitting of fire.

That aroused him fully and quickly to his senses, and starting to his feet, he stumbled upon a revolver which lay upon the floor before him. He picked up the gun and found the barrel warm to his touch, and a wisp of smoke floated in the deep, narrow gullet of the weapon. It was his own revolver! He knew it by four significant notches which he had filed into the handles of it for certain reasons best known to himself.

Startled by this, he stared about him, and then he saw the stranger, Capper, lying on his side against the wall, with a crimson trickle of blood down his face, and an ugly, purple-rimmed blotch on his forehead.

He was dead, and Sherry knew it at a glance. He did not go near the dead body; but he looked wildly about him. There was only one means of escape, but that appeared a simple one—a large window at the farther side of the room. To this he ran. It was locked!

But what was that to Sherry? Outside, he saw the ground; by fortune he had been placed upon the lowest floor of the hotel, and he was a mere stride from freedom.

A hand struck at the door.

"What the dickens is up in there?" asked a rough voice.

For answer, Sherry took his Colt by the barrel and with the heavy butt of the gun he smashed out a panel of the window. A second stroke brought out three more, and a third opened a gap through which he could easily make his exit; but at this moment the door was sent open with a crash.

Sherry whirled against the wall, his Colt ready. It was not the first time that he had had to fight his way out from a tight corner, but apparently the hotel keepers at Clayrock were more thoroughly prepared for trouble than the hotel keepers of other communities. No fewer than five men charged through the doorway, and Sherry, in his first glance, saw a sawed-off shotgun—most convincing of all persuaders—a rifle, and three leveled revolvers.

Courage is admirable, and fighting skill is delightful in its full employment, but even a disposition such as that of Sherry could see that this was not the time to strike back. It was better to be armed with a conscious innocence than to use his gun.

"Stick up your hands!" came the grim order.

And he obeyed quietly.

They found the dead body at once. There was an outbreak of exclamations. They herded Sherry into a corner of the room and took his gun away from him; an armed guard stood upon either side, while the other three lifted the dead man and placed him on the bed.

"He'll never be deader in a thousand years than he is now," pronounced one, whom Sherry recognized as the waiter who just had served him.

"And what'll we do with this bird?" asked another.

"Stick him in jail."

"Why in the jail? Here's his gun warm in his hand! Judge Rope is about good enough for this bum!"

17

"Bill is right," said another. Then: "What you gotta say about this, stranger?"

Before Sherry could speak, a quiet voice said through the shattered window: "If you boys will listen to me, I think I can explain this."

"It's Mr. Wilton," said the bartender, attempting to convey an air of much respect.

They wrenched open the rest of the broken window, and Wilton climbed easily into the room.

"I was half afraid that something like this would happen," said he. "That man is entirely innocent; unless you want to hang a man for self-defense. I knew that dead man. His name was Capper. He sailed before the mast on a ship which I commanded. And when he sent up word to me today that he was in town, I came to see him. He was always a wild, reckless fellow. A little wrong in the head, as a matter of fact. I was afraid that he might get into mischief, and so I came down to take what care of him I could. I even had a drink with him, and it was the drink that polished off the pair of them. When they were carried in here, I wanted to follow, but the door was locked. So I walked around into the garden to look through the window. A very lucky thing that I did! I saw Capper, like a mad creature, as he was, throw himself at this fellow while he was still half conscious. He barely had sense enough to defend himself. You see the bruise on his forehead, where Capper struck him. Capper was a madman. Mad with drink, no doubt. He managed to tear the gun out of the holster of Sherry, here. But that brought Sherry out of his whiskey sleep. He grabbed the gun back and knocked Capper away, and when Capper started to rush in again—he shot him dead."

He made a pause here. Silence and then a murmur of surprise followed this statement.

"Funny, I didn't hear no racket in here," said someone.

"They weren't shouting," said Wilton. "Their brains were too filled with whiskey fumes for that. And, after

18

all, the finish came in about two seconds—before I could get in through the window, in fact! Sherry seemed to come to his senses. He saw the dead body and made for the window, and started smashing it open. He saw, of course, that the case looked black for him, and he didn't know that he'd had a witness who could clear him."

There was a general murmur again; it was of pure assent except for one bearded man, wearing a heavy plaid raincoat. He was a rough customer, with a growth of beard of several days' ripeness upon his chin, and overhanging brows, from beneath which he peered earnestly out at the others. Now he advanced upon big Lew Sherry and stood before him with his legs well braced, and his hands upon his hips.

"Boys," he said, "before you let this gent loose, I want to tell you a few things about him."

"Go on," said the bartender, who seemed to be in charge of the crowd.

But others were gathering, and the room was full of pushing people.

"If a dog bites once," said the man in the raincoat, "you call it bad luck and let him go. If he bites twice, you shoot him, I take it?"

"Go on," said the bartender. "What are you driving at?"

"I'll show you in a minute."

He turned back upon Sherry.

"You know me, Tiny?" said he.

Sherry had worn a dark scowl from the moment he first eyed the other. He hesitated now, but at length he said: "I know you, Jack."

"And how did you come to know me?" asked the other.

"By breaking your jaw for you," said Sherry. "I see you wear a lump on the side of your ugly face still."

The man of the raincoat grinned in a lopsided fashion."

"And how did you come to bust my jaw?" asked he,

19

while all grew hushed with interest, listening to this strange conversation.

"Because you jumped me," said Sherry, "and you well know that you did, Jack!"

"I jumped you," admitted the other. "And why did I jump you?"

"Ah—that's what you're driving at, is it?" asked Sherry.

"It is! Why did I jump you?"

"Because—" began Sherry.

"Listen to this," exclaimed the other.

"Because," said Sherry in repetition, "I killed one of your cousins, and shot up another pair of them!"

An exclamation greeted this statement.

"You hear him?" asked Jack.

"It was fair fight," protested Sherry.

"Mind you, gents," said Jack. "The four of them was in one shack. They'd been felling some timber above the rest of the gang. In that there shack they had the fight. He claims that he killed one of the three and laid out the other two. They wasn't babies, any of those three. I ask you, does it seem nacherel and to reason that he could do it by fighting fair— this gent, mind you, that's just plugged a drunk through the head?"

Sherry looked swiftly around the encircling faces, and all that he saw appeared grim reading indeed to him.

"I got no grouch against this here bird," said the bartender, "but it looks like sense in what Jack says. When a dog bites twice—it shows a habit!"

Sherry searched his mind for an answer, but he found none.

Then the quiet voice of Wilton broke in: "It seems to me, men, that you might ask what happened *after* this shooting scrape at the lumber camp. Did this man bolt?"

"There's a question," said Sherry. "You can answer that, Jack. Did I run for it?"

"You come into camp and bragged about what you'd

done," said Jack. "You come in with a cock-and-bull yarn."

"Did I take care of the two boys that were laid out but not dead?" asked Sherry. "Or did I leave 'em to bleed to death, as I might've done?"

"You come in an' bragged!" repeated Jack, furious at the memory. "I ask you boys to use your common sense. And here you got this gent red-handed. It ain't the first killing. And the one I tell you wasn't the first, either. Here's his gun!"

He snatched Sherry's gun and held it high.

"There's four notches filed in this here. Tell me, was they filed for fun, Sherry?"

He waited, then he answered himself with: "And there'll be five notches in there tomorrow!"

At this, a decidedly stern rumble of anger ran through the listeners. It was after the palmy days of outlawry when gunmen were rather more admired than condemned. Law had entered the West; and the gunman was an unpopular character.

At last Sherry said loudly: "Gents, you're on the wrong trail. This Jack, here, is trying to run me up a tree. I'll tell you the honest truth. There's not a notch there that isn't for the finish of a white man in a fair fight. And that's straight, so help me!"

This speech made an obvious impression, and Sherry could see the effect, as he looked about over the faces of the listeners. He noted that Wilton stood a little apart from the others—or rather, out of an apparent respect for him, the rest would not rub elbows too closely with their superiors. As for Wilton himself, he seemed to be watching this scene as he would have watched something on a stage, in which he had very little concern. There was even a faint smile on his lips, from time to time, as he followed the different arguments.

Jack was not to be downed. "White men?" he exclaimed. "And what else have you accounted for?"

Sherry saw that he had led himself into a corner, but he added quietly, in reply: "I've been in Mexico, boys. And I've had to live in Louisiana among some

21

unpeaceable gents. That's all that I got to say about that."

"It looks sort of black for you, Sherry," said the bartender. "Though I've got nothing against you."

"It's gunna look blacker for him," insisted Jack. "It's gunna look black as choking for him, before we get through with him. This ain't a jay town that's to be buffaloed and talked down by a slicker like this Sherry! He's an educated gent, too. Reads a lot. Knows a lot. How did he ever have to leave home, I'd like to ask? I tell you, if you knew the inside of this one, you'd find it hotter'n cayenne pepper!"

Jack had piled up his points with some adroitness and there was no mistaking the hostile air of the crowd when Wilton interrupted the proceedings again, to ask: "If he came into camp, how did he happen to get off, up there, without trouble?"

"There *was* trouble," said Jack. "But he was the pet of the boss of the show. And that got him off. There was a lot of trouble, but this Sherry is one of those sneaks that always aims to play in with the straw boss, darn him and all his kind!"

This stroke produced another thunder, more thunderous than the rest.

"But suppose," said Wilton, "we find out just what story was told by both sides when they came into the camp that day?"

"The kids told a straight yarn," said Jack. "They told how they'd been sitting around having a little poker game in the evenin'. Sherry lost. Like the yaller quitter that he is, he grouched. They shut him up. He scooped for the money with one hand and begun shooting with the other before any of them could reach for their guns."

"Well," said Wilton, "but isn't it odd that a straight story like that could be disbelieved?"

"Because the boss ran the show and ran it crooked, to help Sherry!" declared Jack. "There ain't much difference between the speed of anybody's draw—hardly a fraction of a second! How could one man do that work against three, and come off hardly scratched?"

The patience of Sherry, which had been fairly well maintained up to this point, now was ended, and he flared forth: "Jack, if you think there's very little difference in the speed of a draw, I invite you—and any friend of yours—to stand up to me inside of ten paces, and we'll start the draw with an even break!"

Jack was so staggered by this proposal that he actually took a backward step.

"One of the three did no shooting at all," said Sherry grimly. "He died while he was lugging out his gun. The second feller got in one as he dropped, and the third got in two. And here's the proof of it. Here's the first one!"

He touched a white scar that clipped the side of his cheek. "Here's the second one!"

He pulled up his left sleeve and exposed a forearm white as the skin of a baby. He doubled his hand, and beneath the skin appeared enormous, ropy muscles, bulging so that they threatened to leap through the skin. Against that setting, turned still whiter by the contraction of the great muscles which stopped the flow of blood, appeared a large purple patch.

"That was the second shot that plugged me," said Sherry. "And as for a third, it's along the ribs of my left side, and it left a mark you all can see!"

Silence followed. Eyes turned slowly to Jack, who protested eagerly: "He could have picked up those marks in any fight. He admits that he had plenty of them, all over the world!"

The voice of Sherry was low and bitter:

"You yellow dog!" said he. "You know that I was dripping blood when I got to camp. And that was why you jumped me. You never would have dared, otherwise. You forgot that my right hand was still ready for you."

Jack bit his lip, and his keen eyes flashed from side to side, seeking for a new idea, but before he could find it, the big man continued quietly:

23

"I told the true story, when I came into camp. We were playing poker. I'd had my share of the luck. It's a lie that says I hadn't. Matter of fact, I was the winner, and a big winner, as things went in that camp. So big a winner that straight poker wasn't good enough for the rest of them. I'd discarded an ace of clubs before the draw. And after the draw I called a hand of four aces! I wanted to argue the point. But the winner went for a gun. I had to beat him to it. And I did. You've heard this mangy coyote yelping at my heels. But I've told you the absolute truth."

Again silence weighed upon the room, and again Jack took a backward step. He had changed color, now.

"He'd be glad enough to see me hanged," said Sherry. "That sort of man hunts in packs, getting others to take the risks that he hasn't the nerve to take for himself. As for this job here, it's a bad one. I'm sorry for it. I'll tell you straight that I had nothing against Capper. I never saw him before today. I don't know exactly what happened. My brain was slugged. I waked up, as you might say, when the gun went off. Then I saw my own gat at my feet, still smoking. And yonder by the wall where you found him lay Capper. Well—it looked black for me, and that was why I tried to run. I've put my cards on the table, boys. There's truth and nothing else in every word that I've spoken. Now, make up your minds."

It was not certain how the crowd would decide, until the bartender stepped forward and confronted Jack. He was not a big man, that bartender, but he was a fighter by nature.

"You!" he said. "This town is kind of cramped and small for your style, I reckon. You'd better blow!"

And Jack blew!

CHAPTER FOUR

THE STRAIN of that impromptu trial had been so great that everyone sighed with relief as the tension relaxed. And now, after having accused Sherry so bitterly, the crowd milled around him in unfeigned good will.

One big fellow slapped him heartily on the back.

"Sherry," said he, "if that's your name, I've got to say that I weigh within a few pounds of you, and yet I've got a chestnut mare at the hitching rack outside that can carry me. If you need that hoss to help you on your way, don't let me stop you from trying to catch up with Jack—the poison skunk! The hydrophobia rat!"

But Sherry waved his big hand.

"That's finished," said he. "I never hunted trouble in my life, and I never will. I never went half a mile after another man with a gun in my hand. And I never will."

A cheerful current of humanity curled closer about him to sweep him down toward the barroom, but he pushed them away with a good-natured might. Then he strode through them, and at the outer door of the hotel, he caught up with Wilton.

Him he touched upon the shoulder.

"I want ten seconds," said he, "to tell you something. I want to tell you that if it hadn't been for you singing out, I might have hung today!"

Wilton smiled and nodded.

"I actually believe that you might," said he. "Our fellows in Clayrock are a rough set. They act first and think afterward."

25

"That's why I thank you," went on Sherry in his quiet bass voice which, however, no matter how softly it was controlled, had a rumble in it like the echo of a far-off peal of thunder. "A few words are just as good as a thousand, I suppose. But you saved my hide. And there's a lot of that hide to be grateful for!"

"By the way," said Wilton, "what was your college?"

Ever so slightly, Sherry started.

"What?" he said. And then he paused and deliberately looked Wilton in the eye. "I don't know what you mean," he said.

Wilton chuckled.

"Of course you don't," said he. "I should have known beforehand that you wouldn't understand what I meant."

"And now that I've thanked you," went on Sherry, "will you let me ask you what you put in that glass?"

Wilton started in turn.

"What I put in the glass?" he echoed.

"Mr. Wilton," said Sherry, "the point is this. I'm no hero at whiskey. But I can hold my share of it. And tonight I seem to have passed out cold in two drinks. That's why I ask you what you put in that whiskey!"

Wilton sighed. His eyes half closed.

"Suppose," he said suddenly, "that you walk up to my house with me?"

"I'd like it fine," said Sherry. "But I can't. For the reason that my bunkie is riding herd for two, just now, and he expects me back."

Wilton answered, with much quiet point: "Nevertheless, I think you should come along with me and I think that you will. Between you and me, Sherry, I confess that you appear to me a fairly reasonable and honest fellow: and if you are, you'll agree that you owe me something."

"I owe you," said Sherry carefully, "for some very opportune remarks during that impromptu trial of me a few moments ago."

"Impromptu?" said the other. "Is that your word for what I said?"

26

Sherry turned full upon his companion. It was a very bright night of stars; and the lights of the town were now few and dim, for most people had gone to bed; and altogether, there was not nearly enough illumination to enable him to see the face of his companion.

"I don't know what you're driving at," Sherry said with a good deal of bluntness.

"You don't?"

Wilton hesitated for an instant, as though many answers were rushing to the tip of his tongue, though he said finally, in a controlled voice: "That surprises me. But I go back to the doped drink. Of course, it was drugged. But what on earth, my dear young friend, could make you think that *I* would drug the liquor?"

"Because," said Sherry, with his usual openness, "you seemed upset because I had taken the glass which you intended for Capper—poor wretch!"

"The glass which I intended for Capper, and which he intended for me."

"What?"

"That's it, exactly. As I put down the drinks, I saw Capper's hand flash over the top of one of them and I thought—I couldn't be sure—that that hand dropped a film of something white into the liquor. What I did definitely see was that Capper deftly exchanged glasses with me. Naturally, I couldn't stand for that. The fellow was half mad, and capable of anything. Between you and me, I should not have been very sorry if he had poisoned himself with his own hand—while intending it for another!"

The voice of Wilton turned hard and grim.

"It sounds a mixed-up business," commented Sherry. "I got the wrong glass as you were slipping it back to him?"

"Exactly."

"It seems odd," said Sherry. "I don't see what point there was in his poisoning you! He acted to me more like a fellow who would be apt to blackmail you—who was holding his knowledge, say, over your head."

"Knowledge?" cried Wilton with a sudden burst of

27

extreme fury. "That gutter rat—that sneaking, paltry, vicious little cur—knowledge of me!"

Sherry was amazed. It was actually the first time that Wilton had so much as raised his voice, during all these singular scenes in which Sherry had watched him; but once the flood broke through, it raged in a torrent.

It was over at once.

"I don't know whether he had anything on you or not," said Sherry. His tone implied that he did not care, either. "I saw him rubbing your nose in the dirt; I watched you taking water from him. Maybe he had nothing on you; anyway, it was darned queer, to my way of thinking."

"Yes, yes," answered Wilton rather hurriedly. "I suppose it was. It was almost as queer an action, say, as that of a man who draws a gun on a drugged and helpless companion and shoots out his brains!"

CHAPTER FIVE

TO THIS startling retort, Sherry listened with wonder and horror.

"We'd better walk up the hill to my house," repeated Wilton.

And Sherry went with him, his brain suddenly benumbed, almost as it had been when he was most completely under the authority of the drug which had been dropped into his whiskey. What hand had dropped it there? The hand of Wilton or Capper? And for what purpose? And now he himself was accused by the very man who had saved his neck from a mob execution.

"You say that I deliberately pulled my gun and shot down a helpless fellow?"

"I tell you what I saw with my own eyes," said the other. "Capper was shot exactly where he lay. He hardly stirred a muscle."

"Great Scott!" gasped Sherry. "Could I have done that, I ask you? What had I against Capper? What had I to gain by his death?"

"A man under the influence of a drug doesn't think along very straight lines," replied the other. "You were in a haze. You still suffer from some of the effects."

"Shot him where he lay—helpless?" groaned Sherry.

"Exactly. There was blood on the wall behind his head, when they picked him up."

"The blood was splashed against the wall in his fall," urged Sherry.

"In the midst of that blood there is a bullet hole," said Wilton. "I think that's fairly conclusive."

He had led the way up a steep incline from the heart of Clayrock, and now as they came before an open iron gate which gave upon a winding driveway, Sherry halted and laid his great hand upon one of the iron pillars that supported the weight of the gate panels.

"I murdered that man while he was lying there?" murmured Sherry.

Wilton did not answer this. Apparently he thought that he had made the case conclusive enough beforehand.

"I don't understand it!" said Sherry. "Great Scott, I don't understand it. Man, man, all my life what I've avoided, as other people avoid death, is any accusation of bullying another person. I've never taken an advantage. I've never fired when a man's head was turned. Heaven knows that I've been low—I've been in the muck—but one thing at least I've always done—I've fought fair."

At this, Wilton laid a hand upon the shoulder of the other and patted it kindly.

"I believe every word you say," said he. "But a drugged man is an insane man. Particularly, people

29

put under by some of those tricky Oriental poisons. And those are exactly what Capper would have used, as a matter of course. And, driven out of his head for a moment, what a man does then is exactly what he would never dream of doing when he is normal!"

"That's clear enough," said Sherry huskily. "That's clear enough and bad enough!"

"It is, isn't it?" murmured the other. "I'm sorry for you, Sherry. I hated to tell you the truth about this, as a matter of fact. But I had to, and for very selfish reasons!"

"Will you tell me what those reasons are?" asked Sherry.

"I've never told a soul in this world," said Wilton. "But the fact is that I'm going to tell you the whole story."

He began to walk up the long driveway.

"Why not tell me here?" asked Sherry.

"Tell you the story here?" cried the other. He laughed with the sudden harshness which, now and again, came into his voice. "Why in the name of caution should I tell you a story where the whole world might listen to me? No, no! Wait till we get to my house. I have one room there that really is private!"

He laughed again, the same jarring laugh, as he repeated this.

And Sherry, amazed, unnerved, sick at heart, went unwillingly up the path beside his companion. The drive doubled twice, cutting along the face of that bluff which he had noticed before rising above the town, and finally it came to the front of the house on the hill which had showed the lights that had seemed as much stars as lamps.

It was not an imposing house. It was built all in one story, and it followed the natural conformation of the ground slavishly. There had apparently been no attempt to level a sufficient space, but the foundations were laid according to the natural contour of the land. The result was an indescribable living line to the upper contour of the building, which pitched up and down heedlessly, like a boat upon the waters, bringing up with a high head upon the northeastern end of the ridge.

"She lies here like a snake, doesn't she?" murmured Wilton.

"Yes," said Sherry in full agreement, "like a snake ready to strike."

He saw the other twist sharply about and glance at him; but now they paused under the face of the dwelling and went directly to that highest spot where the house came to an end. They passed around to the very extreme point, and Sherry exclaimed with real wonder: "Why, it's like the bow of a ship!"

It did, in fact, contract toward that point, so that it gave the whole edifice a strange likeness to a misshapen vessel struggling through the sea. Yes, and in another instant the clay rock seemed a vast wave, which was upholding the ship toward the sky, ready the next instant to dash it to destruction.

These strange images jumped full-grown into the brain of Sherry, and he dismissed them again with a shrug of his powerful shoulders.

"D'you like the place?" asked Wilton in a strangely eager voice.

"You have a view from up here," replied Sherry, noncommittally.

All the plain about them was dotted with the lights of single houses, or streaked with the lights of whole streets. For Clayrock was not a town standing by itself, there were many other smaller villages scattered around it, so that, to carry out the first metaphor that occurred to Sherry, if this house of Wilton were a ship at sea, it was steering by the lights of a most dangerous and twisting channel.

"And now," said Wilton, "we'll go into my room."

He stepped up to the door and turned a switch, which caused a flood light to spring up within. Into the interior, Wilton peered through a small hole which he uncovered and then covered again. After this, he unlocked the door and waved Sherry ahead of him.

"Go first," said he, "and let me tell you that I never

31

go across this threshold without expecting to be met with a bullet through the head or a knife in the throat!"

With this odd introduction, he closed the door behind him, and waved Sherry up a second short flight of stairs that rose from the little entrance hall.

"This is my own private way of coming in and going out," explained Wilton, and unlocked the door at the head of the stairs.

CHAPTER SIX

HE AGAIN waved Sherry before him. "And here is my room," said he.

The illusion of a ship's cabin was almost perfect. The very windows were rounded at the tops, small, and where the chamber narrowed at the front end of the house there was actually a round light! The ceiling, too, was manifestly curved, as though following the lines of an upper deck. To make the resemblance perfect, a narrow flight of steps, hardly more than a ladder with wooden rungs, lifted to a trapdoor out of one corner. Up this went Wilton while Sherry followed him, wondering.

The manner of his host was as matter of fact as that of any man he ever had met in his life, but his words and his ways were odd, indeed! They passed from the ladderlike stairway to the roof of the house. Or, more properly speaking, it was the roof of the room beneath, with little relation to the rest of the building.

The sense that he was in a ship still persisted with Sherry, though now, to be sure, it was more like voyaging through the stars than over any terrestrial ocean.

"I want you to take note of a few of the features here," said Wilton.

And he called attention to the fact that on three sides of the room gave down upon the sheer face of the clay rock, a dizzy fall.

Upon the fourth side, it looked down at least twenty feet upon the nearest portion of the roof of the remainder of the odd building.

"A little fort, you see?" remarked Wilton. "Now, step closer to the edge. Anywhere, closer to the edge."

Sherry obeyed, but with caution. He had a giddy feeling that this singular fellow might thrust him over the side into oblivion! The roof on which he stepped yielded, as he thought, the slightest particle beneath the pressure of his weight, and he heard the faint ringing of a bell from the room beneath. He stepped back in haste.

"What's that?" asked Sherry.

"An alarm, of course. Come down with me again!"

They returned to the room below, and Wilton carried on his methodical demonstration of his house. Sherry listened carefully, knowing that something lay behind all this, but unable to guess what.

"Have you tried the weight of the door?" asked Wilton.

He set it ajar, and Sherry moved it back and forth. It seemed the weight of lead.

And Wilton explained with his usual calm: "There is a half-inch sheet of bullet-proof steel of the finest quality sunk in that door, and in fact, every wall of this room is secured in the same fashion—the ceiling and the floor, too. Those solid shutters which close over the windows are lined with half-inch steel, as well, and the trapdoor leading to the roof. This room, you will see, is such a strong box that if a bomb were exploded under it, it might be knocked off its base, but it would hardly be more than dented by the explosion."

Sherry nodded. He could not help wondering if Wilton were a little mad.

"Now, then," said Wilton, "you will see that it would be very hard for anyone to get into this room, but still, there are drills which would eat through half an inch of steel as though it were soft pine. I can't depend upon steel alone. I need something more, and here it is!"

He set wide a door and revealed a shallow chest where Sherry, with experienced eye, noted at once a formidable little armory.

He saw half a dozen repeating rifles, revolvers, and automatic pistols, pump guns, double-barreled shotguns, and two with sawed-off barrels, terrible at such close range as fighting within the limits of a room.

Sherry examined them with care, and he saw, also, ranged boxes of ammunition for all the different types of weapons.

"You might stand a siege!" said he.

"I might," nodded Wilton.

He opened a second door, and pointed at several tiers of boxes.

"Canned food and distilled water," said Wilton. "Yes, I could stand a siege."

He turned and faced Sherry.

"You want to know why I expect such a thing to happen?"

"Of course," agreed Sherry.

"I'll tell you why. No—it would take a great deal of time. I can't tell you this moment all the details. But after the—"

A bell rang. The ring was twice repeated with a pressing haste.

"That's my niece, Beatrice," said Wilton.

He went to the door and laid his hand upon the knob of it. Then he turned and looked earnestly at Sherry: "She's an unusual sort of a girl, you'll see."

He opened the door, stepping straight back behind the panel, as it swung slowly inward, delayed by its own weight, and Sherry found himself staring into a white, sad face, the eyes surrounded by deep shadows.

A girl came into the room with a graceful step which yet had little lightness in it.

"I've brought you a note, Uncle Oliver," she said.

"Beatrice," said he, "this is Lew Sherry. Sherry, this is my niece, Beatrice Wilton."

She came up to Sherry and shook hands, with one of those casual and forced smiles which Sherry had always hated.

Then she turned back to her uncle.

"This is the thing, Uncle Oliver."

She handed him an envelope. He frowned down at it —then suddenly crumpled it in his nervous grasp.

"Where did you get this?" he asked.

"I'll tell you another time," said she.

"And why not now? I don't mind talking before Sherry."

"Ah," said she, and half turning, she looked with a keenly searching glance at the big man. It was as much as to say: "Have you been enlisted?"

It was to be inferred from her voice and her manner that she was not altogether on the side of her uncle. There was a definite gap between them.

"If you don't mind, then, I'll tell you exactly. I was taking the short cut up the hill—"

"When?"

"Half an hour ago."

"What were you doing out as late as that?"

Instead of answering, she paused, and deliberately looked straight into the face of her uncle.

Then she went on: "I was as far up the path as the place where the old root sticks its elbow out of the ground, and there a hand touched my arm."

"By Jove!" breathed Wilton.

"It wasn't very pleasant. I turned around, and the other arm was caught. There were two men, one held me on each side.

"What sort of men?" asked Wilton, who had turned gray and now sat down.

"I couldn't see. It was pitch black there among the trees. I strained my eyes at them, because of course I

35

wanted to try to recognize them. I think, in addition, that they hadn't trusted the darkness. They had either blacked or masked their faces. So I could make out nothing, except that one of them was about middle height, and the other was a great deal taller. About as tall, I should say, as Mr. Sherry."

She regarded Sherry again, but only for the sake of more accurately estimating his height.

"You tell a story well," said Oliver Wilton ironically. "You never are in a hurry to get to the point, my dear."

"Thank you," she replied, her eyes as dull and dark as ever while they watched her uncle. "I have to take it by degrees. That forestalls questions afterward, you know—if you'll pay attention the first time! I say that I couldn't make them out. I was frightened and—"

"Bah!" broke in Oliver Wilton.

She repeated sternly: "I was frightened."

It was as though she insisted upon the possibility of fear, and her uncle would not allow it in her.

"They gave me this letter," she went on, "and they said to me: 'Tell him that we're straight as a string. With him, too. Only—we want turkey talked!' After that, they let me go. Those were the only words they spoke to me."

"Then how did you know that they were referring to me?"

He asked this sharply, suspiciously.

"I guessed. I don't know how."

She was sneering openly. It was more than dislike that existed between these two. It was actual hatred, as Sherry was beginning to understand. And he considered the girl more keenly than before. She might have been beautiful if her air had been more happy, her eyes not quite so dull, with only flashes of emotion passing through them, from time to time. But a settled melancholy seemed to possess her, and she was faintly frowning all the time.

She had brown eyes; her hair was a very dark auburn. And sometimes, as she turned her head, the red high lights upon her hair seemed to be repeated in the

36

color of her eyes, making a weird effect. Her skin was very white, her eyes unusually large, and the upper lids, when she looked downward, were distinctly marked with purple. Some women make up in this manner to give a touch of thoughtful distinction to their faces; but Sherry did not need to be told that all was natural with her.

He never had seen man or woman at all like her. He put her into a new category and reserved judgment. He was only ready to say one thing: That she possessed as much force—as much danger, say—as any man. And he had known dangerous men!

Another of those unpleasant little pauses had come between her and her uncle. Then she said good night to them and left. Wilton closed and locked the door behind her, and turned back to Sherry.

"That's one reason I live in a steel box!" said he.

CHAPTER SEVEN

IT WAS an odd thing, indeed, to learn that a man's reason for fortifying his room as though it were a block-house is the existence of a young girl. But there was something so extraordinary in the manner of Beatrice Wilton that it appeared to Sherry that there was some justification of the attitude of his host.

At this point, Wilton asked the cowpuncher to sit down.

He said in his quiet way: "You've seen and heard a good many strange things since you came to this house with me, Sherry."

"I have," admitted Sherry.

"I wanted to show you the face of the situation first.

Now, I must tell you why I've been so frank. But first of all, I will give you another bit of testimony."

They went to a clothes closet which was, in fact, large enough to serve as a dressing room, with a small window, like a porthole, opening to the south. From this he came back carrying a gray felt hat, which he held up, and Sherry saw a half-inch hole punched neatly through the crown.

"Air-hole, for hot weather," said Wilton. "Put there by some kind friend—I don't know who. I was walking up the hill one evening and this hat was shot off my head by some man in the brush. I went after him; found nothing. The trees and the bushes make a thick tangle, you know."

"I know," said Sherry.

Wilton, with a sigh as though of relief, tossed the hat back through the door, where it rolled unregarded upon the floor of the dressing room.

"What do you think of this affair, Sherry?" asked the other.

"What you mean," answered Sherry, "is that you're in danger of your life. And I gather that you think Beatrice Wilton may have something to do with your danger. Is that it?"

"That's it," said Wilton. "It doesn't seem possible to you?"

"Miss Wilton, you mean?" inquired Sherry.

"Yes."

"I don't know," said Sherry. "I've been living on the range a long time. You don't suspect women of murder —not on the range. Besides, what has she to gain by finishing you?"

"I am her guardian," said Wilton, "She has a half million or so of property."

"And what of that?" asked Sherry sharply.

"You think I'm a fairly callous fellow?" Wilton smiled. "Well, Sherry, that property goes to her the moment that she marries—or on my death."

Sherry thought this over with a frown.

"You think she's hiring killers to go after you?" he said.

"I don't know," answered Wilton. "My life is endangered. I know that. I know that Beatrice has plenty of reason for wanting to get rid of me. I know that she's not fond of me."

"You're letting me into this pretty deep," said Sherry.

"You want to know how you're interested," said Wilton, "and I'll tell you. I have an idea that during the next ten days there will be special efforts to get at me. During that time I'm going to live under a guard."

He narrowed his eyes at Sherry again.

"You're a fighting man, Sherry," said he, "and I gamble that you're an honest man. Will you take the job of trying to keep me alive for ten days?"

"I had an idea that something like that was coming," said Sherry. "But before I give you an answer I want to know what there is in the job?"

"I don't think," said Wilton, "that one man would be enough. I'd leave it to you to pick out some other good fighting man, some reliable fellow. You can pay him whatever you like. And I'll pay you—a thousand dollars a day."

Sherry frowned.

"You don't like that?" asked Wilton curiously.

"A fee like that," said Sherry, "is almost too big to be paid for honest work. However, I'll think it over. Tell me, Wilton, if you suspect any other person beside your niece?"

"I suspect every living soul around me," said Wilton in his calm way, which he retained even when saying the most startling things. "I suspect even you. You may have been planted somewhere at the hotel so that I could fall in your way. Yes, I suspect everyone."

"Why should other people want to get at you?"

Wilton considered, his glance fixed upon the ceiling. "I don't think I'll answer that," said he.

He looked straight at Sherry, and suddenly the big

fellow realized that his host was a man capable of anything—certainly capable of banishing all shame.

"You want me to watch over you," answered Sherry,
"but at the same time you want to blind one of my
eyes. Is that very logical?"

"I can tell you this," said Wilton. "If ever sailors
come near this house, be on your guard against them.
Outside of Beatrice, the next danger that I know of
has to do with the sea. Someone from the sea, Sherry,
is going to take a try at me."

"Someone like Capper?" suggested Sherry.

"Like Capper," nodded the other. "But a great deal
more formidable. Capper was a good deal of a fool.
Bloodthirsty. Exactly that! I mean to say: he was so
interested in making trouble that he hardly cared if he
ruined himself in making the other fellow suffer. However, I expect that we may have a visit from a more
dangerous sailor than Capper!"

"And that's all that you can tell me?"

"I can tell you a little more than that. There are
several sets of people that want me to die."

"Within ten days?"

"Yes, within ten days."

"Your niece is one of them?"

"When her father died," said Wilton, "he left her
money in trust for a year. At the end of that time, the
control of her money was to pass into my hands, if
I cared to undertake the work of guardian. That work
meant giving up my own affairs entirely. But I de-
cided to make that sacrifice."

He looked straight at Sherry, and the latter looked
straigt back at his host. There had been a little ironical
intonation on the last word.

"And the sailors? You can't tell me why they're
after you?"

"No, not a word about that."

"You don't know how these people might try to
come at you? Guns, you say?"

"I don't know," replied Wilton. "I'll tell you some
of the things that I'm half suspecting: Poison adminis-

tered in food, with a blow arrow, or perhaps through the bite of a snake. Or again, there's something to be feared from the thrust of a Malay knife. And, of course, I've already had a bullet through my hat."

Sherry shrugged his shoulders.

"Why shouldn't you close yourself up in your steel box, here, and pretend that you're being besieged for ten days. You have everything you need."

"I have this place," said Wilton, "because I can sleep here with a slightly greater sense of security. But no place is completely safe. Suppose a bomb loaded with poison gas were thrown through a port into this cabin, one night?"

"They'll do anything to get at you?"

"They'll do absolutely anything!" Wilton assured the cow-puncher.

Suddenly he rose to his feet. For the first time he betrayed a real emotion.

"There are people that I know of," said he, "who would sell their souls for the sake of shooting me through the head. Do you understand?"

Sherry nodded. Under those last words there had been an electric thrill of hysteria; and Sherry understood, in a startling burst of insight, that the calm of Wilton was totally affected and unreal. It was a calm surface with a storm beneath.

"Well," said Wilton, "you've heard as much as I can tell you. What do you say to this proposal, Sherry?"

"A thousand dollars a day," repeated Sherry. "And for the sake of that, I'll have to get a partner, and then the pair of us will have to go on guard—and the moment we start work, we'll both be targets for the same hands that are aiming principally at you?"

"You will, of course."

"Well," said Sherry, "the money—and the fun—interest me!"

"You'll take the place?"

"Yes."

Wilton sat down at a table and scratched a letter. Then he rose and passed it to Sherry, who read:

41

Riverside National Bank,
Mr. H. A. Copley.
Dear Mr. Copley: If I am alive ten days from this date, please pay ten thousand dollars to Lewis Sherry. If I am dead, destroy this letter.

Your very truly,
Oliver Wilton

"Will that do?" asked Wilton.

"Of course," replied Sherry. "When do I come up here?"

"At once!"

"We're driving in a bunch of beef tomorrow morning at dawn. By nine o'clock I'll be here, and I'll have a man with me."

"That leaves me another night," muttered Wilton, "with only my own pair of eyes to keep watch. But I suppose that I'll have to!"

"I'm going back to camp, then."

"At nine tomorrow?"

"I'll be back."

"Good night," said Wilton. "And if this talk keeps you awake tonight, don't waste your time—spend it cleaning your guns, because you'll need them before you finish working for me!"

CHAPTER EIGHT

EIGHTEEN HUNDRED steers, dismayed by the sight of many houses, the snorting of a locomotive on the railroad, the intricate, strong fences of the cattle corrals near the station, filled the air over Clayrock with booming and bellowing; and as Lang and "Tiny" Lew

Sherry looked at the lashing tails, and listened to the clashing of the horns, Lang said:

"Now, Tiny, we've done our job, and if you ain't particular hostile to the idea, I'm gunna let the watches run down while I lubricate my innards. The thirst that you were talkin' about the other night is a dog-gone lake of sparklin' spring water compared with the charred wood and the white ashes inside of me. Just gimme a steer to the layout you found, and—"

"Drop it," said Sherry, with a grin, "you're just getting ready to work."

Pete Lang, recoiling his rope, stopped his hands to look at his friend.

"Have you been exposed to the sun, partner?" he asked. "You ain't scrambled your brains like a plate of eggs, I hope?"

"For ten days," said Lew Sherry, "you're not going to so much as look sideways at liquor; you're going to keep to a desert trail and thank heaven for water when you can find it."

Pete Lang finished the coiling of his rope and tied it in place.

"You got a terrible saddening influence over me, Tiny," said he. "Now what do you want?"

"You," said Sherry, and told him the complete story of his exploits in Clayrock—the strange death of Capper having already been described, as a matter of course. But now he went on to the details of his talk with Wilton, and the odd proposal which Wilton had made to him.

"Now, how do you size it up, partner?" asked Lang.

"I don't know," said Sherry. "Except that I know you and me are going to go up there and take that job."

"Do you know that?" murmured Lang. "You know a brainful, then; and you got a long start on me. But what sort is Wilton?"

"I don't know," said Sherry.

"Is he a crook?"

"There's a large chance of that. Otherwise, he would have told me why the sailors are after him, no doubt."

43

"Is that your only reason? Why, Tiny, this gent is a hard-boiled skunk, most likely. He's probably so mean that he could live on jerked coyote with cactus thorns for dessert. You're still young, Tiny; and now you just foller along with papa and leave Clayrock when I leave."

Sherry shook his head.

"Why, Tiny," exclaimed the cowpuncher impatiently, "it's a crooked frame. This Wilton is probably going to be bumped off, and you want to be in on the digestion of the bullets. Is that the way that you figure it?"

"Five thousand a piece for us, and ten days to wait," said Sherry. "Doesn't that sound to you?"

"Like funeral music, it sounds to me, Tiny."

He pushed his horse closer and tapped Sherry on the shoulder.

"It ain't the coin that pulls you in," said he.

"What is it, then? The trouble?" grinned Sherry. "Am I being drawn in by the chance to chew lead, old fellow?"

Pete Lang reined his horse back again.

"I never seen a puncher made high, wide, and handsome like you, Tiny," he remarked, "that wasn't a hit with the ladies. The bigger they come, the harder the girlies steps up and slams them. A little man like me," said Pete Lang, looking down regretfully on a wiry body not more than a shade under six feet in height, "a little man like me," he repeated, "has always got a streak of meanness in him that saves him from tons of trouble. By the look of the bait the wise wolf knows the trap. That's me, big boy! But a poor bison like you comes along and steps in and breaks off both legs at the knees."

"Are you accusing me of being drawn into this by the girl, Pete?"

"Nothing but!"

"A girl actually likely to do a murder, old boy? Do you think that my tastes run in that line?"

"There's only two things necessary for a girl to have: youngness and a pretty face."

"I said nothing about her face. I only told you that she seemed tired, with circles around her eyes."

"If she hadn't been a beauty, you never would have noticed the shadows," declared Pete Lang. "Kid, keep away from that Wilton and all his crowd. He's a bad actor!"

"You've never laid eyes on him," said Tiny with some anger. "Why do you talk so much about a man you've never seen?"

"I can see him in the corner of your own eye," answered Pete Lang. "You've already been thinking the same things that I've been saying. Isn't that true?"

"Let me alone, will you?" cried Sherry. "Confound it, are you afraid to tackle this job with me?"

"Scared as a rabbit!" replied Lang, with the heartiest earnestness. "I don't want any part of that bet! You come on with me and chuck the girl. Besides, she's got too much money to be good!"

"What do you mean by that?" demanded Sherry.

"Never give a starved dog too much raw meat," said Lang.

Sherry laughed.

"You've got to come along with me," said he.

"Not on this trail, kid. My way leads toward moisture."

"Well, so long, then."

"Are you dead set?"

"Yes."

"So long, Tiny. We've rode a good many trails together. I hate to see you barging off. But bullets and poison and knifes makes too big a shadow for me to see the girl that's under it all."

They shook hands, and presently Sherry had jogged his horse back up the street and swung it gloomily around the corner, in order to head toward the house on the cliff. It had been a great disappointment for him to part with Pete Lang. Of all the men he had met in the West, no one had been revealed to Sherry as so keen a fighter, so true a friend, so keen an eye upon the

45

trail—all qualities which in the house on the cliff seemed likely to be tested.

He had reached the first bend of the road leading up the cliff when hoofs clattered behind him, and Pete Lang drew rein at his side.

"You'd 've let me go," said Pete. "You cold-blooded fish, you! You'd 've let me slide, an' heaven forgive you for it. But I was made with a heart inside of me, and so I've got to foller along after you!"

"Old boy," answered Sherry, "I was never gladder to see any man's face."

"But," cautioned Lang, "I told you before and I tell you now. This is a bum steer that you're following. You're drifting in a blizzard, kid, and I only hope that you don't hang us both up on barbed wire!"

To this, wisely, Sherry made no answer. They approached the gate of the Wilton place.

Before it, Lang drew rein again.

"We gotta go in here?" said he.

"Yes," said Sherry. "This is the place."

Lang sighed.

"Well," said he, "there's no writing over the gate to tell us what kind of trouble we're going into. Make a noise, cayuse, and scatter up that gravel!"

With that, he whacked his pony with his quirt, and the mustang, with a snort, fled through the gate and up the winding way, the gravel and dust flying like smoke beneath the hoofbeats.

Sherry followed at a more leisurely pace, so that he found his friend already dismounted, and tethering his horse to the hitching rack before the house. He followed that example, and heard Lang muttering: "I never seen a house in my life that looked like more trouble!"

Beatrice Wilton came out of the house in a wide-brimmed straw hat, with a gardener's trowel in her hand. She paused near Sherry, and he looked at her with a fresh interest; for the strong, bright sun, seeping through the thin brim of the hat, tinted her skin with rosy gold.

"You've come to stay, I take it?" said she.

"I think I have," said Sherry, and he introduced Pete Lang.

"And you, too?" asked the girl, looking straight at the cowpuncher.

"I foller along with Tiny," answered Pete Lang. "If he rolls his blankets here, I suppose I stay along with him!"

She swung her glance back to Sherry.

"I think that you'll make Uncle Oliver feel quite safe," said she, and with a nod to them, she went off down the first walk of the garden.

Pete Lang looked after her and then grinned at his friend.

"And that's your girl with the shadows under her eyes, is it?" said he.

Sherry sighed.

"I didn't remember that she looked like this," said he.

"You're a young liar, son," said Pete Lang. "But I'm here to make a statement. You got no chance with her. She's a thinker, me boy, and none of her thoughts are gunna be about you, unless she finds you in the way. Now, let's go in and see the gent in the trap!"

CHAPTER NINE

THEY FOUND Oliver Wilton fairly quivering with excitement in spite of the strict control which kept his voice steady. He could speak evenly enough, but he could not keep his hand from shaking. He made a brief examination of Peter Lang.

"You're a friend of Sherry's?" he inquired.

"We've daubed ropes in the same outfit for a spell," was Lang's characteristically oblique answer.

47

"You shoot straight, Lang?"

"I can hit a mark if it ain't too small," said Lang.

Wilton did not smile. He turned sharply upon Sherry.

"Is this a first-class fighting man?" he asked.

"First-class!" said Sherry, emphasizing both the words.

"You know him?"

"I'll tell you how I met him—" began Sherry.

"Never mind," said Wilton with a sigh. "If you trust him, I can. And you haven't come too soon, Sherry. Have you talked to Lang?"

"I've told him every word that you told me."

"Before I agreed to him!" exclaimed Wilton, flushing with anger.

"If he hadn't stayed, I wouldn't have stayed," answered Sherry. "And as for repeating what we hear, we don't talk for our living."

"No," said Wilton, his teeth clicking together. "You're going to fight for it; and you can begin fighting now. I've had word from the hotel that there's another ruffian down there talking about me. His name is Fennel. Joe Fennel, he calls himself. He tells people in the hotel that he doesn't have to work for a living. He declares that he knows enough about me to make me keep him in luxury for the rest of his life."

He raised his clenched fist shoulder high and his face contorted with rage for an instant. Then the hand fell as he controlled himself again.

"I want you to find out about that man," said he.

"I won't be very popular around the hotel," said Sherry.

"On the contrary, I gather that the crowd is all for you. I think I arranged that little matter for you, Sherry!"

Sherry nodded.

"Find Fennel and talk to him. Don't let him know that you come from me. Try to see if the fellow is real or a sham. Here's the doctor now. He's been telling me about Fennel!"

A tall man came into the room. He was partly bald

—a premature baldness which, in fact, accentuated his youth, for he could not have been much past thirty years of age. The baldness, too, made his brow appear the more lofty; it was the commanding feature of his face—a great and swelling forehead which made him look an intelligent giant. He was introduced as Doctor Eustace Layman, and he shook hands with a firm, crisp grip.

"I was repeating what you told me about Fennel," said Wilton.

"He's a drunken old scoundrel, who spends most of his time in his room, soaking up whiskey behind locked doors," said Layman. "He's a sailor and he's certainly a bad actor."

"I'll persuade the hotel to throw him out as an undesirable," suggested Wilton angrily.

"I wouldn't," replied the doctor. "I don't think they'd do it. He seems to have plenty of cash and doesn't care how he spends it! Besides, if you pay too much attention to him, people may think that there's something in what he talks about. I mean—that he knows something black about you!"

"How do you happen to know so much about him?" asked Wilton. "You seem to have him by heart!"

"Because I've been called in to see him. He almost had a fit the other day."

"Fit? I wish he'd strangle in the course of it!"

"Too much alcohol—that was his trouble. Depressed heart action and subnormal temperature—that sort of thing."

"How far gone is he?" asked Wilton with an eagerness which quite broke through his usual easy manner.

"He'll last indefinitely," said the doctor. "He's a tough fellow. A real old sailor, and bad weather seems to line them with leather, inside and out!"

"Will you go down to the hotel today?" asked Wilton of Sherry. "Will you try to see the old rascal and find out about him? I'll show you your quarters first. After you've made yourself at home, perhaps you'll go down and look things over."

49

Sherry agreed; and with Pete Lang he was shown to their quarters. They could not have been more confined if they had been in the steerage of a ship, and in fact, nothing could have been more like a cramped cabin than their room, which was lighted by the round ports which Wilton affected, and which had a built-in bunk on either side of a narrow passage. It lay just underneath the room of their employer, and as they stowed their luggage, Sherry asked his friend what he thought of the lay of the land. Peter Lang paused in the smoothing down of his blankets.

"We're riding herd on a new range, kid," said he. "We gotta take time to find out the natures of these steers. All I know is that there's gunna be trouble!"

When they were fairly settled, they went down together to the hotel and almost the first person they found in the cardroom was their man. He looked the perfect part of a hardy sailor. His skin was like mahogany; around the cheekbones it had a polished, ruddy look, while the lower part of his face was clouded with unshaven brush. At the very moment of their entrance, Fennel was heard calling for a drink in a husky voice, as one whose vocal cords have been strained and frayed by constant shouting against the scream of the westerlies.

Lang said aside to his companion:

"I'll start talking with this fellow. You get a chance to slide up to his room. Get into it if you can."

"If the door's locked?"

"If the door's locked, that may block us for today. Make a try."

It was not hard to find the room of Fennel on the hotel register; and Sherry went up to it at once. It lay at the end of the southern corridor on the second floor of the hotel, and luckily the hall was empty as Sherry passed into it. He tried the door—it gave at once to his hand, but he paused, with a chill working through the muscles of his back. He had been in many an unpleasant situation; he had had to fight his way through many a tight corner, but never before had he gone unlawfully into the room of a stranger.

So, half guilty, and half determined, he waited for an instant until he remembered the seamed face of Fennel, and then he pushed on into the chamber.

It was a little corner room which had two windows; but both of these were closed and the air was foul with the stale fumes of bad tobacco smoked in some ancient pipe. The chambermaid had not yet made up the bed, and Sherry told himself, with a sneer of disgust, that the sailor must have slept all the night in such an atmosphere.

On the wall facing the bed, in such a manner that the sailor could see it the last thing at night and the first in the morning, was a picture of a clipper ship. It was apparently an enlarged photograph of old standing; the edges were splintered or furled by much wearing, and there was a visible crease across the center of the picture. Still it was a stirring thing, for it showed the clipper before a gale, leaning dangerously in the wind, and yet holding onto a main skysail with a dogged persistence. Such a picture must have been taken from the poop of an ocean liner as it crossed the bows of the sailor; and it showed Sherry the very leap of the waves, the very straining of the cordage.

He admired that picture for a moment only, and saw the inscription under it: "*Titania*, Outward Bound!"

Somewhere he had heard of her—a queen of the tea fleet, and afterward a sturdy veteran, lugging merchandise from England to the western coast of America, and always a flyer.

However, he had other things to think of. Perhaps Fennel had sailed on the *Titania*, but that was only a small bit of information. He pushed up a window softly and opened the shutter a crack. It was not a great distance to the ground, and for a good athlete, there was a drainage pipe running down from the gutter of the roof above, straight past the window to the earth.

So, having established that in case of need the sailor could be reached from the outside of the hotel, Sherry closed the window and shutter and turned back to the room itself.

Everything was in disorder. On the bureau lay a belt containing a large sheath knife, several blackened, cracked pipes which looked as if they had been smoked in many a gale at sea, so eaten was the wood by the fire; there was a blue-and-yellow handkerchief; a pocket knife with a roughened horn handle; a tattered newspaper, and several boxes of matches. On the corner table stood two whiskey bottles, one nearly empty and the other quite gone. Beside them was a tumbler. The top of it had been broken off, and the fragments glittered on the floor.

All a miserable confusion, but doubtless order enough to please a man who might have spent most of his nights in the forecastle of a ship.

Last of all, Sherry saw a sailor's chest of strong three-quarter-inch pine, all dovetailed, painted black, with brass drop-handles, and a two-inch rising board beneath. It was not locked. He lifted its water-tight top and looked in.

Most of the things, he was surprised to see, were new, and of cheap, heavy coarse stuff, such as a sailor might be expected to take to sea with him. Fumbling through it, Sherry noted a feather pillow, cot blankets, canvas shoes, a pair of knee-boots with pegged soles, plate, basin, quart and pint pots of block tin, a house-wife containing needles and thread—heavy and coarse and strong—mending wool, scissors, and tweezers. And all these things were new! However, there was a pair of very battered working boots without any nails in the soles or heels; and these were indeed so extremely battered that Sherry wondered at finding them with the rest of these comparatively new goods; the soles, for instance, had been worn completely through.

There was nothing else to see in the chamber. He left it in haste, and returned to Lang, below.

CHAPTER TEN

ALTHOUGH IT was not late in the morning, Fennel already appeared to have an excellent lead, and as Sherry entered, he was singing, or attempting to sing, an old chanty of the sea. But fog filled his throat, and his breath came with a wheeze and a sputter. Nevertheless, some rhythm remained:

"There's a saucy wild packet—a packet of fame—
She belongs to New York, and the *Dreadnought's*
    her name,
She is bound to the westward where the strong
    winds do blow—
Bound away in the *Dreadnought* to the westward
    we'll go.

"Now the *Dreadnought's* a-sailin' down the wild
    Irish Sea,
Her passengers merry, with hearts full of glee;
Her sailors, like lions, walk the deck to and fro—
She's the Liverpool packet—O Lord, let her go!

"Then a health to the *Dreadnought* and to her
    brave crew,
To bold Captain Samuels and her officer, too,
Talk about your flash packets, *Swallow Tail*, and
    Black Ball,
The *Dreadnought's* a flyer that can lick them all."

If the voice of Joe Fennel was almost totally inadequate for the singing of this ballad, still he rendered it with such life, and at the end smashed his hand so heavily upon the table that even the bartender, a sour man, could not help smiling.

"Another shot all around," said Joe Fennel to the barman, "and smart's the word! There's your mate. Come here, kid, and sit down!"

Sherry joined them at the table. The whiskey was brought.

"This round is mine," said Sherry.

"I say no!" coughed Fennel, spilling a handful of silver on the table. "Take the price out of this, and keep the change. Free and easy is my life, lads. I got no call to go aloft again, like a fly into a spider's web. Some works by their hands, and some by their heads— and some," he added with a sinister joy, "by the pickin' up of information. And that's the ballast that I sail with now. Information, hearties! You couldn't see my Plimsoll line, I'm so deep with it! Talk has been paid for before now, and silence'll be paid a long sight better. And if you doubt me, ask the squire that's got the house on the hill!"

He paused to drink, and then cough and laugh.

"I'm sendin' up a boy with a message for that skipper that I'm gunna tell him to have his wallet all shipshape and Bristol fashion because I'm gunna review it! He's been law and lord on blue water. But I'm gunna be law and lord to him on dry land, as sure as ever a ship wore the name of the *Princess Marie!* As sure as ever a ship wore the name of the *Princess Marie!* Another shot all around! When I speak, run, steward. This ain't a sailor's home!"

Sherry stood up.

"I've had enough," said he.

Lang rose beside him.

"Are you takin' in sail at the first squall?" demanded Fennel. "Never take in sail for a squall that you can look through. Ain't you men enough to see light through a shot of grog?"

They waved their adieus to Fennel in spite of this urgent plea, and as they left they heard him ordering two bottles of whiskey which he went off carrying under his arm.

The face of Lang was contorted with disgust and contempt as they got into the open.

"It's enough to turn a longhorn like me into a temperance preacher, kid," said he. "The low-down skunk! Drinkin' by himself, paralyzin' himself slow and gradual in his room! Think of it, kid! Think of it, Tiny! It's gunna make me give up red-eye!"

Sherry thought of the broken glass and the bottles he had seen in the sailor's room, and he nodded his assent. Then Lang asked him what he had found in the room of Fennel. He listened with the keenest attention.

"New clothes, did you say, Tiny?"

"New, cheap stuff."

"And old boots?"

"The soles were as thin as paper. The leather of them was rotten, if ever I saw rotten leather. They were so old, Pete, that the folds of the leather were hard and brittle. I scarcely can see how a man could put on boots like that!"

Lang was so struck by this that he paused and laid a hand on the shoulder of his friend.

"As old as that!" he said in wonder.

"As old as that," nodded Sherry. "What do you make of it, Pete? After all, there's nothing so very strange about a pair of old boots. I've had them myself!"

"In a sea chest! In a sea chest!" insisted Lang. "I tell you, that's the point, old boy. You never been to sea!"

"Have you?"

"Well," said Lang, deliberately giving that question his shoulder, "I'll tell you what—it's a dashed funny thing. Old boots and new clothes to rig up a sea chest!"

He shook his head and walked on, so deep in thought that he looked like a man in pain. At this, Sherry no longer bothered his companion with questions, for he knew that Pete Lang, absorbed in thought, was like a python struggling to assimilate some gigantic meal. A strange fellow was Pete Lang. No one ever had come to the bottom of his nature; but a more useful man upon the trail to handle the problems thereof, Sherry never could have found. He began to look to Lang already, as to a man capable of working a miracle.

Pete Lang said at length: "I'll see! I'll see!"

He spoke rather like an impatient father, teased by questions, although as a matter of fact, Sherry had not said a word. And so they returned up the hill to the house of Wilton and found him in the garden with his niece. From a distance they heard his voice in a hard tone of irritation, speaking rapidly. Only in brief pauses could she have answered. They could not hear her voice, until they came out of the brush, and then they heard Wilton come to the fiery end of a sentence and heard the girl say distinctly, quietly: "No!"

It was a sort of key to all that had gone before. He had been storming at her about something, and she had been holding the fort of discussion with that single word: "No!"

"You won't reason!" exclaimed Wilton. "You won't listen to reason at all. You don't want to hear me!"

"No," said she, "I don't!"

It amazed Sherry, he slowed and would have halted, but Lang took his arm and forced him on. They heard Wilton exclaim with greater emphasis than ever: "And what, under the name of heaven could I possibly have had to do with it?"

To this she returned no answer at all, but pointed toward the two who were approaching. Wilton faced about on them with a start. And Sherry saw the girl watching them with the keenest curiosity. Then she turned and went off in haste. Looked at in full face she appeared a worn and weary woman, indeed, but as she went off, with the turn of her neck and the lightness of her step, she looked more child than woman—a happy, careless child.

This thought of her made a great impression upon Sherry, for he was one of those men who do not reason

56

very closely, who cannot go with mathematical precision from premise to premise, but with bursts of intuition his mind leaped ahead, as though a light had been cast on the future. So he saw Beatrice Wilton with new eyes, and wondered at her—and at himself!

Wilton was vexed, plainly.

"How long have you two been standing there?" he asked.

"We ain't been standing," said Pete Lang.

Wilton waved a hand, as though he would have said that he doubted this, but the point was not worth further discussion.

"You fellows have learned to walk silently, while riding the range," said he. "Now, what do you want?"

He corrected himself with a faint smile.

"I forgot that you've been doing my errands. You found the man, did you? You found Fennel, as he calls himself?"

"We found him. We had a drink with him," said Sherry.

"You drank with him!" cried Wilton. "But I wouldn't do that, if I were you!"

"How does he look?" asked Wilton.

"I'll show you," answered Lang.

He took out a pad of paper and a stub of soft pencil; with that he rapidly worked up a sketch, as Sherry had seen him do a thousand times up the range when his swift hand would jot down things big and small—the line of mountain against the sky—a hunch-backed cow with tail to the blizzard—a coyote, lolling a thin tongue and laughing at the ranch dogs. Or perhaps it would only be a Spanish bayonet, distinguished for peculiar uprightness—or a close-up, as it were, of the dreadful thorns with which the cactus is armed. With half a dozen sweeping lines Pete Lang could show you a mustang bucking, a rider just lurching up from the saddle, out of balance. And so he now worked on the face of Fennel, the forehead covered close to the eyes with matted hair, the odd bulge of the forward part of the head, and the lower features masked with the scrub of beard. In that half-minute of work he even was able to impart to this sketch the evil sneer of Fennel, the peculiar and working malice.

"By Jove, I know him!" exclaimed Wilton under his breath, as he peered at the paper.

Then he shook his head.

"He's a liar. He never was one of us," said Wilton.

"One of who?" asked Sherry innocently.

His reward was a keen, stabbing glance.

"What did he talk about?" asked Wilton.

"About the value of silence," answered Sherry, "which he said you would certainly pay for—as surely as ever a ship wore the name of the *Princess Marie!*"

The hand of Wilton froze in mid-gesture. Then slowly he raised it to his face. He looked like a man who had been struck by a mortal bullet. And so, without another word, he turned and went slowly toward the house.

CHAPTER ELEVEN

NOW THAT they were left alone, Sherry stared after Wilton for only a moment, when he turned to Lang and said quietly; "Guilty, your honor."

"Guilty as sin," said Lang. "Guilty of what, I wonder. What's this dirty rat Fennel got on Wilton? What's Wilton done in the South Seas that you read about? I tell you what, kid, I'm beginning to get red-hot about this! I'm beginning to get red-hot all over! And I'll never leave the trail until we've run it into some sort of a corner! Wilton guilty, the girl looking like she had fire in the hollow of her hand—the dickens is to pay up here, Sherry, what with the steel-lined room, and the rest!"

"Let's take a walk and think this thing over," said Sherry. "I never think so well as I do when my legs are moving."

"It keeps the blood stirred up," grinned Lang. "You think like a wolf, kid—with your teeth!"

However, he strode off at the side of Sherry, and they pushed back through the woods that grew close behind the house of Wilton where big spruce and pine were commingled.

"How do they ever get rain enough to keep them going?" asked Sherry.

"Where does the water come from to make this run?" countered Lang, and he pointed to a trickle of water so small that it made a mere silver gleam, winding along upon the ground.

"Where from?" murmured Sherry.

"You got no eyes," answered the puncher. "You can have a whole spring jumping out of the top of a hill, if there's other higher ground anywhere around to send down the rain water. Look at them mountains over yonder—ain't they catching the rain and filtering it down through the strata? And one of them strata turns up here like a leaky pipe and lets out some water. Hey kid, this is real country!"

The clay rock, so narrow and slender that it rose above the town like a raised hand, now spread right and left and grew into a considerable plateau; the surface was very broken; the trees did not always stand straight, but jutted at considerable angles, at times, from the irregular surface of the land.

"This would make a first-class hole-in-the-wall country," remarked Lang. "You could hide up twenty men, out here, and they could thumb their noses at everybody that tried to find them. Look around, kid. Was there ever in all the world a better country for a murder?"

Sherry agreed with a nod, for they had come out from among the trees, at this moment, and found themselves at the edge of a bluff at least two hundred feet high. Just at its base the river curved close in. Sherry kicked a stone clear of the edge and they saw its dizzy drop, its disappearance, and the sparkling leap of the water around its fall, like the spring of a fish.

"Tap a gent on the head here," said Pete Lang, "and drop him where that stone dropped, and you'd never hear much report about him. Look where the water gets white!"

Racing along the base of the cliff, the water hardly showed the speed of the current, except that it was dark instead of limpid; but at a little distance farther from the town, the current struck rocks that jutted above the surface like the prows of swift ships, each spurning a bow wave, and covered with spray.

"That machine would eat a man pretty small," suggested Lang, and Sherry agreed with a grunt.

They walked on. The surface of the ground grew more and more broken. It was chopped across the face by many small ravines, deep as a man, and sharp-sided.

"What's the good of carrying on here?" asked Sherry. "Walking is one thing, but climbing is another. Why you can't talk at this work, let alone think!"

"You'd make a good general!" said Lang ironically. "You'd fight in the dark!"

"Fight?" queried the big man.

"Tiny," exclaimed the other, "you make me tired! You make me ache! Ain't we here fighting for our lives?"

"I don't follow that exactly," said Sherry. "We fight to save the life of Wilton, as I make it out—and instead of keeping an eye on him, here we are, rambling away through the woods!"

"If we didn't live under the nose of a tiger," said Lang, "d'you think that he would pay a thousand a day? Ask yourself that, old son!"

It made Sherry glance briskly about at the trees.

"And if that's the way of it," went on Lang, "we ought to know the lay of the land out here!"

They went on in silence; in fact, it was such hard work that there was little opportunity for talk until at length something crackled through the branches over their heads. Lang stiffened, attentive.

"What the deuce was that?" asked Sherry.

"You shut up!" cautioned his companion.

He had delivered that advice in a whisper, and now he commenced to stalk forward with a catlike agility, pausing from time to time. In one of those pauses, distinctly though faintly, Sherry heard a soft thud, such as might be made by an ax with a sharp edge, shearing through a tough green branch.

Presently, peering around the corner of a large pine trunk, Lang beckoned Sherry to his side, and the big man looked around at a very odd sight.

In the center of a small clearing stood Beatrice Wilton, with a revolver in her hand, and even as Sherry looked she took quick aim, swinging the gun smartly up from the hip, and firing. The dim spurt of smoke was the only sound to tell that a bullet had been discharged —that and the same dull, quiet thud which he had heard before. He understood it now. It was the impact of a small-caliber bullet entering the trunk of a tree. A silencer appeared on the muzzle of the revolver.

To Sherry there was something wonderfully grim in the appearance of the girl, her mouth set firmly, determination in her eyes—the very poise of her body showed that she was practicing for more than mere game!

Twice more he saw her fire, and each time the bullet struck home in a small sapling not more than six inches in diameter.

Then Lang waved Sherry back, and they stole away through the woods and back toward the house, with a painful slowness.

When they were on the edge of the trees, again, with the house partly outlined beyond them, Sherry asked: "What do you make of it, Pete?"

"You talk sad and you talk small," said Pete. "It sort of riles you, kid?"

"Why should it?" protested Sherry.

"Why shouldn't it?" snapped Pete Lang. "You get yourself all heated up about a girl—and then you see her practicin' with a silencer on a gun—and hittin' the mark—and lookin' as though the mark was a man. A silent gun's a murderer's gun, Tiny!"

Sherry groaned.

"I've nothing to say," he admitted. "But I want to ask you what—"

"Don't bother me," said the cowpuncher. "I gotta think, don't I? For myself, and Wilton—and you, you poor snowblind cayuse, you!"

They went on toward the house, and coming out into the garden they saw, on her knees in a bed of flowers, busily at work with a trowel, a big garden hat shading her face, no other person than Beatrice Wilton herself.

She looked up to them with a cheerful smile.

"Have you been wandering around in the woods?" she asked.

"To see what the lay of the land was like," answered Lang, for Sherry was dumb with amazement.

"They're grand old trees," she replied. "And Uncle Oliver won't sell them!"

They went on past her.

"Nice gent, that Wilton," said Lang. "She's sure gotta be grateful because he ain't sold the old trees off of the place!"

"What does it mean?" asked Sherry. "How the dickens could she have come back here before us, old-timer?"

"She knows the woods! There may be level ways, if you know the angles and the corners. That's not what bothers me!"

"What in heaven's name does, then?"

"The cool way of that girl. Cool as ice, Tiny. But no coolness under the skin. She looked after us all the way until we got around the corner of the house!"

"How did you tell that? I didn't see you look back."

"I felt her look. She's got that kind of eyes!" said Lang.

They went to their small room, and they hardly had settled down in it before their employer tapped at the door. He invited Lang to "go up with him to the office," while Sherry stretched out on his bunk to piece together what they had learned.

Presently both Lang and Wilton came back; Wilton was pale with anger and excitement.

"Sherry," said he, "I think that I'm paying you boys well. I've offered to double that pay if one of you will get rid of Fennel for me. You understand? I'll double the money. It'll be twenty thousand dollars on the nail! Lang, here, refuses!"

"I don't follow that—entirely," said Sherry slowly. "One of us bumps off Fennel. Is that it?"

"That wouldn't stop us," broke in Lang with an odd glance at his companion. "It ain't the first man that Sherry, here, has slipped a slug into. But you gotta hold your horses, Wilton."

"I tell you on my honor," said Wilton gravely, "that that man may ruin me!"

"If he's the real article?"

"Real article?"

"Not a fake, I mean."

"How could he be a fake? He knows already—"

"He's a darned actor," said Lang with conviction. "Did you ever hear of a sailor with a whole new outfit —and one old pair of sea boots—with holes in the bottom of 'em? A fine comforting thing a pair of boots like that would be, going around the Horn!"

"By heaven!" exclaimed Wilton, and quickly struck his hands sharply together.

"And how long ago," said Lang, "did sailors stop callin' whiskey and rum grog? He's a fake!"

CHAPTER TWELVE

THE REACTION of Wilton to this strange remark was odd, to say the least. He glared hard at Lang and asked sharply: "Have you been at sea?"

"I ain't spent all my days on the range," admitted Lang.

Wilton continued to regard him with distinct disfavor.

"You haven't spent all of your days on the range, eh? How did you sail?"

"Before the mast."

"Where?"

"And what's that got to do with the job here?" asked Lang bluntly.

The fist of Wilton balled suddenly. Then he controlled himself.

"You're sure that Fennel is a faker?"

"As sure as I'm standing here."

"Lang, there's a good deal depends on this!"

"By the way you carry on, I suppose there is," replied the cowpuncher.

Before Wilton could make further remark, there was a loud rap at the outer door.

"Will you open and see who's there?" Wilton asked Sherry.

So Sherry went to the front door and opened it for Doctor Eustace Layman, whose usually pale face was now flushed from walking up the hill. He came in upon them with a wave of his hand in greeting.

"I've been called in to see this fellow Fennel," said he. "The rascal is drinking himself into an early grave."

"I wish he were under the sod already," commented Wilton. "Is he seriously ill?"

"Typical alcoholic. Subnormal temperature; jerky hands; dull eyes, and a sinking in the pit of the stomach."

"What did you do for him?"

"Told him to stop all liquor at once. The rascal simply cursed the world of doctors, and poured himself another drink under my eyes. After that, he gave me a letter to carry to you."

"A letter for me?"

"Here it is."

Wilton received it. "It seems the scoundrel is a sham," he said to the doctor. "Lang saw through him. Lang has been at sea!"

"A sham!" murmured Layman, and looked askance at Lang. "Are you sure of that? He appears like the real article, to me! He's low enough to be really in the part!"

"He ain't so low as all that," said Lang. "He's got a brain in his head!"

"Did you guess that by his talk?" asked the doctor.

"By his eye," answered Lang. "You can change a good many things, but you can't keep thought out of a gent's eye."

"Ha?" said the doctor. "You're a clever fellow, Lang! I can see that!"

Wilton, in the meantime, was tearing open the envelope.

"He's printed the letters," said Wilton. "He wouldn't trust his handwriting, it seems!"

Then he gasped, and suddenly crumpling the letter, he thrust it into his pocket, as though he feared that some hand might snatch it from him.

"What's upset you, Oliver?" asked Layman. "If the fellow's a fake, how can he trouble you like this?"

Wilton slowly drew out a handkerchief, and dragged it across his forehead. He looked white and sick; in fact, he had to lean one hand against the side of the door jamb.

"He's coming here," said Wilton. "He's coming here some time this afternoon, and he invites me to meet him in my garden, Eustace!"

"Nonsense," replied the doctor. "Make him meet you in your room, of course. Or rather, don't see him at all—if Lang is right about you. What's to be gained from talking to a mere sham and—"

"You talk like a fool!" exclaimed Wilton. "I've got to meet him. This afternoon— I'm going up to rest, now. Will you go up with me, Eustace?"

They went together out of the little chamber of Sherry and Lang and climbed the stairs. On the way, Sherry could hear Layman making some suggestion, and to it Wilton answered in a loud and angry voice: "I tell you, I won't have any more of the stuff. Either I'll have a good, normal sleep, or else I'll get on without it altogether!"

The door of the steel room closed behind them, and Sherry sat down heavily on the bunk nearest him.

"My head's spinning," he confessed. "If this rat Fennel is a sham, how can he upset Wilton like this? Why should Wilton plan to see him at all?"

Lang did not answer, and Sherry continued: "Why didn't you tell me that Fennel was a sham?"

"What good would it do to tell you? What good? The thing you tell is the thing that you've lost. I gotta few ideas already in my head about these people. But if I tell you, then they'll die. Telling a secret is killing it at the root. You can throw the reins and dismount, old-timer. I'm gunna drift this herd if I can, and you can't help me, much!"

Even this bluntness did not disturb Sherry, who stretched himself on the bunk and folded his hands under his head.

"I'm not a clever one like you," said he. "You can do the thinking for the party; call me when I'm wanted."

And instantly he closed his eyes and pretended to sleep.

"You ain't a man, you're an ox," said Lang. "You

were made up of nerve and muscle and bone, and the brains left out. I would rather——"

Sherry heard no more, but slept in fact until he was wakened by a dimly heard tap on the door, and then by the squeak of the hinges as it was opened.

Eustace Layman came in to them saying: "You boys may find Wilton a little trying for the next few days. The truth is that he's upset and his nerves are frayed very thin indeed. I want you to bear with him, if you can."

"We're paid for that," replied Sherry.

"You're paid well," replied the doctor, "and for my part, I think that you're paid for nothing."

"You think that?"

"Wilton's imaginaiton is running away with him. I never knew an old sailor who wasn't apt to have more daydreams than were good for him, and I believe that's the trouble with my friend Wilton."

"Is he an old sailor?"

"He was on the sea for years. Became a skipper, in fact."

"Did you ever hear of a ship called the *Princess Marie?*" asked Lang.

"Great Scott, yes," said the doctor, "and so has everyone else who knows anything about the Wiltons!"

"How come that, doctor?"

"Why, that was Everett Wilton's ship, of course," said Eustace Layman. "The one that foundered in the typhoon."

"Foundered?"

"Sprang a leak in a heavy wind and went down."

"I don't recall hearin' of any such a thing," said Lang. "Not while I follered the sea, and I used to hear a good deal about the China Seas, and that part of the world."

"You know that bit, eh?"

"Pretty fair."

"She was only two thousand tons, but she was a new, strong boat. She was such a good one that Everett put his brother in command of her, because he didn't want to trust any other person with such a large part of the Wilton fortune. Well, she struck this typhoon of which I was speaking, sprang a leak, and went down. Twelve of the crew in two boats made Hevavo. You know that port?"

"Yes, in San Cristoval."

"The ship was a clean loss, and she wasn't insured for half her value, and the cargo wasn't insured at all, I believe. It was a hard blow for the Wilton fortune. It cut the Wilton money in half, I should say!"

"And that was the *Princess Marie!*" murmured Lang.

"That was the ship. She was only six months old. Everett had great hopes of her. I've always thought that it was the loss of the ship that made him so despondent."

"Made him sort of low, did it?" queried Lang.

"Low? Why, man, you know that he committed suicide?"

"Suicide?" cried Sherry, springing up.

Doctor Layman drew back a step.

"Suicide, of course!" he said with a slight frown. "He made sure of himself by jumping off the bluff into the river. The rocks nearly cut him to bits—but there was enough left for the purpose of identification."

"Suicide!" muttered Sherry. "How long ago?"

"Nearly a year."

"No wonder his daughter is half a wreck!" said Sherry grimly. "I'm glad that I've heard this."

"One runs into these melancholy temperaments," said Layman. "It's in the Wilton blood, of course. Strong-tempered people; never can quite tell what they'll do!"

He turned toward the door.

"You'll bear with Wilton, boys, for a few days?"

"Of course," said Sherry.

The doctor nodded cheerfully to them and went out. They could hear him whistling blithely as he walked away from the house into the garden.

"Cool fellow, eh?" commented Sherry.

"Cool?" said Lang. "He's too cool. I don't like him

worth a cent, I can tell you!" Then he added: "It's a fine job that we've got into. I'd rather ride herd on five thousand mavericks than try to handle this job!"

"Suicide—shipwreck—it's a fine job—you're right! But you won't chuck it, Pete?"

"Have you still got hopes for her?" asked Lang with brutal suddenness.

To which Sherry replied calmly: "Of course I have, old son. She's walked into the middle of my brain and I'll never be able to get rid of the thought of her!"

CHAPTER THIRTEEN

THE AFTERNOON came on chilly and dark; the wind lay in the northwest, with the sting of the higher snows in it, and carrying black clouds which looked as though they were about to drop a cargo of rain over Clayrock in passing; but as they spread southward, the darkness departed, and they sank over the south horizon in droves of milk-white fleeces. Under this sky, Wilton sent forth his two guards, saying briefly: "Look over the garden. Print the paths in your brains. Come back here in an hour. I'm going out to meet Fennel!"

He said it with a desperate quiet, like a man full of his hate. And Sherry and Lang went out and leaned against the wind, which, leaping straight across the valley, smote the great clay rock with a constant volleying.

Three paths opened from the house. Sherry took one, and Lang another, and they strode off on their exploration. Pausing at every juncture of paths, Sherry tried to make careful note of them all, but he found that he was having very little luck. There seemed to be two systems employed in the layout of the paths through the Wilton garden. On the one hand, there were two winding paths which worked up the hillside with gradual curves, to make the ascent more easy. On the other hand, there was a much briefer way of ascent or descent, and that was a path which dropped in sharply angling zig-zags to the foot of the slope. All these paths intersected here and there in the most random fashion, for the garden had not been laid out in any methodical pattern, but the paths had been made for the sake of conveniece to get up and down the hill. Sometimes the two curving ways crossed one another and recrossed; sometimes the path of descent cut sheer across the others, turned abruptly, and dropped again toward the foot of the rock. Sherry, work as he might, could not untangle this confusion and bring the scheme to any order in his mind. He even lost the main ways two or three times, and found himself in some little clearing among the trees, where the Wiltons had laid out bright scraps of flower gardens in their random way.

The second time he entered one of these, Beatrice Wilton sprang up from a rustic bench on which she had been seated, her head resting on both hands, and out of her lap something dropped with the bright glitter of steel to the ground.

She stepped hastily forward—as though she hoped that with her feet she could hide the thing. But Sherry shook his head.

"I saw it," he said.

She waited for an instant, as though about to reply; but then she apparently changed her mind and stopped and picked up the revolver. She slipped it inside her jacket and faced Sherry again with a defiance as distinct as it was silent.

It roused a little impatience in his mind; he pointed toward the hidden weapon.

"Why do you carry that?" he asked.

"We have rabbits here," she answered. "One gets a whack at them, now and again."

"And you have a silencer on it, too."

"Of course. That's to keep from scaring the other rabbits."

"Let me see the gun," he demanded.

She paused.

"Well——" she consented. And she held out the revolver unwillingly.

It was of a very small caliber, but specially made in every respect, with a long, delicate barrel, on which the silencer looked oddly out of place. When Sherry broke the gun open, he found that it was loaded with long .22s. He shut it again with a snap. Then he handed it back to her.

"You don't like it," said she.

"No," answered he. "I don't go in for murder!"

Even as he spoke, he felt that he was being foolishly blunt and rude, but he was hardly sorry as he watched her eyes widen at him.

"That's a great deal to say," she observed. But he saw that she was not angry. She was rather frightened, and her face was full of suspicion. "But I know," she went on pleasantly, "that you fellows from the range don't stop to pick your words. At any rate, you know well that one has to learn to take care of oneself in this part of the world."

"No woman does," he told her.

"And why not?" she asked.

"Because the men look out for them, of course. You're a Westerner. You know that better than I do!"

"I understand you now," she replied. "Western chivalry! But I know the truth!"

"Look here," said Sherry. "Why don't you come out in the open? Maybe I could help."

She turned her head away a little, and he knew that she did so to cover a faint smile of derision, or of doubt; but that hardly mattered so much as the new view he had of her in profile. For from that angle, he saw no longer the shadows of trouble about her eyes, nor the pain, which stiffened her lips. At a stroke she seemed five years younger, delicately and purely lovely.

He, rather breathless, went blundering on: "I see

71

what you think. You've heard yarns about me in the town. About the killing of Capper. I'll tell you straight. There was something in the whiskey; and it drugged me. Whatever I did, I don't remember it—any more than that bench remembers anything. Do you believe that?"

She looked back at him, as cool as any man.

"You're here as a fighting man," she said, "and Uncle Oliver doesn't make mistakes."

"I've done my share of fighting," he admitted. "But I don't apologize for that. I never hunted trouble in my life."

"You simply stood where it was sure to come; you stood and welcomed it?" she said.

He raised his head and looked at the clouds shooting in close-mustered ranks out of the north.

"Well," he replied thoughtfully. "Perhaps you're right about that. I haven't thought about it in that way. However, you'll admit that I know something about guns."

"Yes. Of course."

"Then take my advice. Throw that gun away. Give it to me now! No good will ever come to you from that sort of a revolver! It'll never kill a rabbit, though it would easily kill a man!"

He watched her with dread as he said this, and his heart sickened when he saw her flinch.

"Will you do that?" he pressed. "Will you give the thing to me? And if it's merely protection of some kind that you want—protection against what I can't tell— why not let me take on the job?"

She, for an answer, held both her hands away from her, palms up.

"You'd never understand!" she said. "And heaven knows it's something that I can't explain! I daren't explain it even to myself!"

Sorrow and doubt of her so filled the heart of Sherry, that he scowled upon her for a moment, and then he said: "I've warned you. You'll find out that I'm right!"

He turned about on his heel and went off—but

slowly, for he yearned to hear her calling him back. But she said not a word, and when he reached the circle of the trees and looked back at her, she was sitting on the bench once more, with her head in her hands.

The hour was nearly over, and, therefore, he went slowly back in the direction of the house. He would have been lost if it had not been for the occasional glimpses he had of the white façade through the trees. But by their help he was able to correct his course several times and at last he came out on the more level ground before the Wilton house. Lang at the same moment stepped from among the trees, his head down, as if he were heavy with thought. He hardly glanced aside at his friend as Sherry hurried up to him.

"Can you make out this queer place?" he asked Sherry.

"I found the girl," said Sherry hastily, "sitting among the trees with that murder gun in her lap. She talked oddly, Pete, I can't make her out. What in the world is happening in her mind?"

"The dickens is loose all around here!" muttered Lang for an answer. "But I'm going to study it out—I'm going to study it out!" he declared more resolutely. "I only wish that we had a few days more time. But we're pinched for time, Tiny! We're mighty pinched for time! They're all wrong; they're all crooked, and yet we gotta try to read them!"

When they came to the house itself, Wilton stepped out to meet them. He had put on a heavy overcoat and muffled his neck in a scarf. Nevertheless, he trembled, and he explained his shuddering by saying curtly:

"I'm too long off the sea; every cold snap sends a chill through me! We're going down the straight path," he added. "Fennel will be somewhere along it, I think. And now, boys, you understand what I'm facing, don't you?"

"A pile of trouble," said Lang, "and you're a fool to run yourself into such danger. There ain't any need of it!"

Wilton made an impatient gesture.

73

"I didn't bring you here to be judges of what was best for me," he said angrily. "I brought you both here as fighting men. Do you hear? When I walk into that garden today, I'm walking into peril of my life! I expect you to be close to me—close behind. If so much as a leaf stirs—shoot, and shoot to kill!"

He added by way of a spur: "You get your money if I live through the ten days. You don't get a penny, otherwise. Follow on close behind. Do you hear?"

They nodded, and he walked on with a brisk but uncertain step, as though his legs had become weak at the knees and his feet had no feeling of the terrain.

Behind him went the two guards, Lang muttering to his companion:

"He's never going to walk back, Tiny!"

Then they turned the first angle of the path, and saw Wilton stiffly halted, and before him, half lost under the shadow of a pine, and leaning against its trunk, the tall form of Fennel. He was laughing in silent content; a most gruesome grimace.

CHAPTER FOURTEEN

"WE'D BETTER close up on him—Wilton is scared pretty near to death!" said Pete Lang.

So, with Tiny Lew Sherry, he advanced to the side of their employer. Still the drunkard sailor—if sailor he were—leaned by the tree and laughed at them, until it became hideous, impossible to watch him. For it seemed as though he were mocking all three, like some devil beyond the reach of human strength or malice. And yet here were three armed men, mature, strong, capable of hard battle—and yonder seemed only a shaken rag of humanity. It was the unreasonable laughter that made the man appear so terrible.

"Stay close to me," muttered Wilton hoarsely as the two came up. Shame was actually driven from him. He kept his eyes fixed upon the nondescript form of Fennel, enchanted with terror. "I'm afraid to be alone near that man, Sherry. You stay close to me! You, too, Lang. If I ever get through this, I'll make you know my gratitude!"

At this last moment, Lang still attempted to argue.

"Look here," he said, "what's the good of this? You know that he's not a real sailor. He's lying. He's simply trying to blackmail something out of you. Why be a fool like this? Let me go and tell him to get out of this. You don't have to talk to him at all. I wouldn't, if I was you!"

Then Wilton, in spite of fear—or because of it, perhaps—turned in a fury upon the other.

"Look here, you," he said, "I tell you that man knows everything! I've hired your hands, not your wits. Do as I tell you!"

Sherry stared at Wilton. It was hard to think that the man was sane, yet making such richly implied admissions of guilt as this. In fact, he saw that Wilton was *not* sane. His common saving sense was swallowed up completely by blank fear.

However, now Wilton was facing forward toward the enemy, and he went ahead with a quick, light step, which certainly belied the state of his emotions. Or perhaps it sprang from the desperation of one who wanted to have this suspense ended, no matter what the cost might be.

Fennel did not leave his tree as the trio approached him, but remained leaning against it, still laughing, so that the sound became audible—a husky wheeze, rather than normal human laughter. A beastly imitation of the human sound. He wore an ancient and faded felt hat, was wrapped to the throat in a tightly buttoned overcoat that dragged almost to the ground, and on his feet were partly visible wrinkled boots, like those which Lew Sherry had seen in the sea chest of this seaman, or pseudo-sailor.

When they were very close to him, at last Fennel left the tree and advanced toward them a few steps, entering the path, but with a staggering step. The man appeared very drunk. Even the upper part of his face was darkly flushed.

Wilton halted as the fellow approached him.

"He never was aboard, but I know him," Sherry heard him mutter plainly thinking aloud. "*Where* have I seen him before?"

Then Fennel, having drawn close enough, said in his thick way: "You think I'm gunna talk to you when you got your pair of bulldogs with you, eh? Dashed if I am! I ain't gunna talk to you at all unless they fall back astern a half cable length, say!"

Wilton hesitated. Twice he turned back toward his companions, and twice he faced again toward Fennel, at last he snapped over his shoulder: "Fall back, boys. Fifteen or twenty steps, say. D'you want to walk on with me, Fennel?"

"You an' me side by side, like old friends, which we are or ought to be," said the rascal. "You and me together, skipper, like the good old days!"

With that, he actually took the arm of Wilton, while Sherry looked on with disgust and wonder. The pair drew ahead; they were almost around the first bend, when Sherry and Lang started to follow, Lang saying: "Dashed if I like this. I don't like it at all!"

At fifteen or twenty paces it really was rather hard to follow the two through such a labyrinth as this garden, where the paths twisted and dodged so unreasonably, but by the sound of the voices they were guided on their way—by the voice of Wilton, rather, for that of Fennel, husky and obscure, was lost in the wind.

"I don't like it," reiterated Lang.

They almost stumbled on top of the pair, at the next turning of the path, for Wilton and Fennel had halted and Wilton was expostulating in a rapid voice, with many gestures that had both fear and appeal in them.

When he saw his guards behind him, he caught the arm of Fennel and drew the man rapidly ahead, as though it was even more to his interest than that of the sailor to be free from observation.

Twice again Sherry had view of the couple, and all the time his sense of guilt of Wilton was increased; every glimpse of the man showed that he was in a blue funk—because of the presence of such an obvious reptile as Fennel.

They came next around a sharp corner into that straighter path which went down the face of the slope with only a few angles in it. They could look straight before them for a hundred yards, but now there was no sign of either Wilton or his companion.

Lang gave Sherry a signficant glance, and they hurried ahead. Lang had his revolver in his hand now, but Sherry still kept his under cover. He was a more practiced warrior than his friend.

They had at least a partial explanation of the disappearance of the other two, the next instant, for they went blundering past the hidden mouth of a narrow path, adjoining. Up this they turned and went over two windings of it. Then Lang held up his hand; they both halted; not far away there was a rustling through the brush.

"Go get it!" said Lang. "I'm going to hunt around here! Go get it and bring it back!"

Sherry hesitated, not as a man depressed by fear, but rather as one gathering himself for a spring. Then he leaped away into the trees. He had spotted the rustling, faintly crackling noise that he had heard; and now he made toward it with all his speed, swerving around the broad trunks of trees, dodging this way and that, and still sweeping invincibly toward the place from which the sound had been audible.

He almost overran his quarry. Had the face been turned away, he would have plunged past the bush, but that white glimmer of skin warned him just as he was springing by. He whirled in midstride, a trick learned only on the football field or in the squared circle of the boxer, and, gun in hand, lunged straight in upon—Beatrice Wilton!

As a lion takes up a cub, so he took her out, by the nape of the neck—so to speak, and held her up.

She was utterly white. She was trembling in his grasp. The revolver with the silencer on its narrow muzzle hung helpless, almost shaking out of her hand.

"I didn't do it!" she stammered at Sherry. "I swear that I didn't do it!"

"You didn't do what?" he asked her.

Then he saw something on the other hand.

He turned it up. The palm was smeared, the fingers were thick with crimson.

"Blood!" exclaimed Sherry.

She, herself, held that hand before her face, saying stupidly, in a mutter: "I didn't do it! I didn't do it!"

The lips of Sherry compressed and his nostrils expanded. He took the gun away from her, none too gently, and found the barrel warm. He opend the cylinder. One bullet had been freshly discharged and the empty shell remained. A faintly pungent odor rose to him. Burned powder, of course!

Then he took her firmly by the arm.

"You're coming back with me," he said.

She drew in a gasping breath. He had heard exactly that sound once before. It had been in a Mexican drinking place, and the gasp had come from a man who had received a knife thrust in his heart.

"I can't go," said Beatrice Wilton.

"Why not? What've you done? Whose blood is that?"

He snapped the brief questions at her.

"I don't know—mine, perhaps," she said.

"Are you hurt?" he asked her, more savage with grief than with angry suspicion, even.

"I don't know," she whispered, and began to shake violently again. "Only—don't take me back there! I couldn't stand that—I—"

"You've got to come. Or else tell me why!"

He urged her forward, as he spoke, and she turned up a pale, sick face of fear and horror to him.

"Please! Please!" she begged.

Lew Sherry picked her up in his arms and she made no resistance, but her head rolled helplessly over on his shoulder. He glanced down and saw that her eyes were closed, though her fists were tightly clutched.

So he bore her back in that arm, straining with the weight of her, but with his other still armed hand fending off the branches. He came close to the path and there he paused.

He said huskily: "Listen to me! If you've done something, if you want to dodge it, tell me what you've done. Then I'll take you away. I'll take you so far that you'll never be found. I'll—I'll look after you. You understand?"

He thought she did not hear, at first. Then she opened her eyes at him, but not with understanding, only with sick trouble.

Sherry choked, and because he did not know what else to do except obey the original instructions of Lang, he carried her tenderly out into the narrow irregular pathway.

He saw Lang at once, kneeling in some tall grass near the verge of the path, and suddenly the girl twisted in the arm of Sherry and pressed her face hard into his shoulder. He was beside Lang, now, and looking down among the grass he saw a man's body lying face down. At that very moment Lang turned the body face upwards and exposed the white, troubled features of Wilton himself!

He had been shot through the head. There was a very small purple spot between the eyes, and a very thin trickle of blood ran down over the right eye and onto the right cheek, where it disappeared in a blur.

CHAPTER FIFTEEN

AS BEATRICE WILTON, half fainting, leaned against Sherry, he lowered her to the ground. Pete Lang stood over her.

"Miss Wilton," he said, "d'you know anything about this?"

"No! I only know that I—I stumbled over the body!"

"Did you see the sailor? Fennel, I mean?"

"No!"

"Did you stop here?"

"Here? By Uncle—"

"Yes. Did you stop here?"

"No, no!"

"You went straight on past him?"

"Yes, yes!"

"You'd better go back to the house," said Lang.

"I'll go," she agreed.

She looked up to Sherry with the same appeal in her eyes that he had seen there before; then she moved away. But still, at a little distance, she turned again, and flashed back to Sherry a wild glance of appeal.

Sherry remained, staring at his friend, and Lang stared back at him.

"What became of Fennel?" he asked. "He must have done this!"

"Fennel? I dunno!" muttered Lang. "Look here, kid. Is there apt to be two .22-caliber, high-powered revolvers in the same town at the same time—both of 'em with silencers on their guns?"

"She couldn't have done it," protested Sherry,

though he knew that his voice was weak with the lack of conviction. "She simply could not have done it! You know that, Pete. Tell me you realize that!"

Pete Lang grunted savagely.

"She lied straight off the bat," he pointed out. "How could you want me to talk soft about her, eh? She lied like a streak. She didn't stop near the dead man. You heard that?"

"Well, and what about it?" asked Sherry.

"Well, man! Didn't you see the blood on her hand?"

"Brush is full of thorns," said Sherry desperately. "You take a young girl like that—let her see a dead man—and what will she do? Bolt, of course! No looking where she's going! And the result will be blood on her hand, if she scratched it on a thorn. You see that, Pete? Of course you see that there's a lot of sense in that?"

Pete Lang looked upon his friend with an air of pity.

"I'm kinda sorry for you, Tiny," he said. "That's all that I got to say to you. I'm just kinda sorry for you. Now, we'll leave things be. The sheriff will want to see this, without too much of the scene changed. You scatter down to town and let the sheriff know about it. And then head straight on for the hotel and take another look at Fennel's room. It ain't going to be hard when they know that he's suspected of murder!"

Sherry was very glad indeed to have something active to do. He made no protest against the manner in which his friend had taken the lead in this affair, but like a good lieutenant, he marched unquestioningly to obey orders.

He got his horse at the stable behind the house and went down the steep road to the street in one furious plunge, with a rattle of flying gravel before him and a rolling of loosened stones behind.

It was easy to find the sheriff. He sat like a wooden image in front of the hotel, staring unwinking before him and occasionally smoothing his fine white beard. Sheriff Herbert Moon never drank and never smoked.

He had no nervous need of occupying his hands with trifles and his brain with a cloud of smoke. He ate little. He talked less. And he held down his office of sheriff not by dint of popular speeches or appeals to friendly voters, but by sheer brilliance in his office, wherein his record was flawless and unequaled during these past twenty-five years. Exactly half of his life he had spent in catching criminals of all kinds. The work had made him look at least fifteen years older than his actual age. But still he stuck to his task. Nothing changed. He hated change, men said, and that was why he remained in Clayrock, living in the same little shed which had served him as a youth, twenty-five years before, and propping it here and there, from year to year, as its knees grew weaker, and its pathetic back threatened to break. He never had married. He never had so much as looked at a woman. He had no friends. He lived, in fact, incased in solitude, like a sword in a battered but strong sheath. But when there was use for the weapon—lo, the pure, bright flash of the steel when it was drawn!

So with Sheriff Herbert Moon, who sat at rest, all passive, resting in body, in mind, and in soul, until the summons came which brought him out upon the man trail.

In twenty-five years, he had killed or captured two hundred and twelve criminals single-handed.

In that list there was no account taken of the sweepings of drunkards from gutters in the early days of the mining boom. But two hundred and twelve times he faced danger for the sake of upholding the law, and he had nearly always won.

It was said that for every year of his service in Clayrock, Sheriff Moon carried a scar. Some silver dot or streak upon his body for every one of twenty-five years of labor! But his face was unmarked. Only, below the chin, there was a long, puckering slash. He was ashamed of it. He always muffled his neck with some sort of scarf, so that he was given rather an old-fashioned appearance by this peculiarity of dress; and indeed, it was merely to harmonize with that necessary neck-mask that he had allowed his beard to grow, and had trimmed it slender and narrow. If his neck apparel was old-fashioned, so should all his appearence be.

Time, from the moment that he made those two alterations in his appearance, made but a gradual change in the sheriff. Only, each year his attire seemed more threadbare. Men declared, mockingly, that he never had bought a new suit of clothes for twenty-five years. Some men vowed that he was a miser, and that he must have a fortune stowed away in some corner. However, not a soul was aware that the salary of the sheriff had stood still for a quarter of a century. No one thought of increasing it. The buying power ôf the dollar dropped to thirty per cent. But the sheriff asked for no raise of pay and none was given him. Of the rewards which he earned by his courage he took no account, but always gave the money, as it came in, to charity.

"A man cannot live on blood money, you know," said the sheriff.

To this little man—"He's so small, that's why he don't get shot up bad," said the tough citizens of Clayrock—to this little sheriff, on the veranda of the hotel, appeared big Lew Sherry. He leaped from his horse. A billow of thin dust swept before him as he halted in front of Herbert Moon.

"You're Moon? You're the sheriff?"

"That's my name, sir," said the sheriff.

"Wilton's been murdered in his garden. I came along to report. He was shot through the brain. The body's lying where it fell. Pete Lang is waiting to show you everything."

The sheriff stared, for an instant, his lips parted. Against the white of his beard, those lips seemed young and smooth and strangely red.

"Dear me, dear me!" said the sheriff. "Wilton is dead! Another rich Wilton, and in a single year. Dear me, dear me!"

He did not rise at once. He continued to look at Sherry as though the big man had told him the most remarkable thing in the world.

"I'm going to tell you one thing more. The man that did the shooting was Fennel—the drunken sailor that lived here in the hotel and talked so much and drank such a lot more," said Sherry.

"I'm glad to know that," nodded the sheriff. "Of course I want to know who did the murdering. Thank you, Mr. Sherry."

"You know me?"

"Of course. Since the day you killed Capper. I've known you ever since that day. I have to know people who can shoot so straight," said the gentle voice of Herbert Moon.

It made Sherry feel a little uneasy. We like to read the character of a new event in its face. We don't wish to go by opposites. This fellow appeared to Sherry like the most inoffensive of men. He looked like a learned man, tired of study, retiring from his labors.

But he was a famous warrior. He was not one who had killed a great many. After his first month in office, he had not had to. Men usually surrendered when this terrible and quiet little man came upon their traces. But he almost frightened Sherry with his gentleness.

"Are you going back with me?" asked the sheriff.

"No. I'm going to stay here, just now."

It occurred to Sherry that he had better not announce his intention of searching the room of Fennel. That might interfere with the sheriff's ideas of what was best. And most desperately did Sherry want to conduct that search in person, in the hope that, in some fashion, he could be able to fasten upon the sailor the crime of that day.

For there was ever, in the back of his brain, the image of Beatrice Wilton, with the blood upon her hand.

In his own pocket was her gun, the silencer attached, the empty cartridge! He felt that that was her destiny; and he carried it; he would guard it!

He went into the hotel and said bluntly that he

wanted the key to Fennel's room. The clerk, impressed by this sternness, handed it over without mark, merely staring, and Sherry went up to the chamber.

It was exactly as it had been when he last saw it. But there were four whiskey bottles upon the table instead of two. Three of them were empty. But the forth was still untouched.

Suddenly Sherry struck his knuckles against his forehead. He turned. The clerk was in the doorway, a little frightened, but very curious.

"Has any one been in this room drinking with Fennel?" Sherry asked.

"Nobody," said the clerk.

Sherry stared at the whiskey bottles again. It was most odd. According to the mute testimony of those bottles, Fennel had consumed more than a quart of whiskey in his room since Sherry last examined the place. But that was not possible. What, then, had become of the liquor?

A small matter, no doubt, but when there is murder in the air, small matters loom large.

CHAPTER SIXTEEN

"IS THERE anything wrong?" asked the clerk.

"Murder, that's all," said Sherry gloomily.

He enjoyed, mildly, the confusion and the astonishment of the other.

"I knew that no good ever would come out of a rat like that. I never seen such a fellow for absorbin' whiskey. A couple of quarts a day, sometimes. I never seen anything like it! He was a regular sponge," declared the clerk.

A sponge, indeed, if two quarts of whiskey could be consumed in a single day!

He brooded upon the problem and upon the room, and as though to get more light on the subject, he opened the window nearest to the table.

"You take a man with a brain full of alcohol, that way, he'd be sure to do pretty nearly anything. Crazy with drink, day and night. Sometimes you could hear him laughin' and singin' in his choked way here in the room in the middle of the night!"

Sherry listened with only half his mind. The other half was fumbling vaguely, as a man will do at a problem in geometry, when all the lines and the angles go wrong for him. And in that state, he stared at the drainage pipe that ran down the wall and noted with dim unconcern that a spot on it was of different color from the rest, fresher, as though it had rusted less. He touched that spot, and it gave on hinges to his finger. It was, in fact, a trapdoor let into the pipe. It brought Sherry quickly out of his haze. What was that used for?

He stared more closely. He could see that the edges of the metal had been cut not long ago. It would not have been a difficult task, for the pipe was lead.

Then a thought came to Sherry, and he hurried out of the room and down to the garden to a point just below the window of Fennel's room. The clerk was leaning out the window.

"Find anything, Sherry?" he called, with eagerness.

Tiny Lew stood still, his eyes half closed, his breath drawing deeply. But there was no mistaking the odor which welled up thick and rank from the ground all about the vent of the drainage pipe. Close about it, the grass was brown and dead. It had been soaked with alcohol poured down the pipe. And that was the meaning of the trapdoor in the drain! That was the explanation, too, of the Herculean drinking of this sham drunkard.

"Find anything?" exclaimed the clerk again.

"Not a thing," said Sherry, and went straightway to his horse and cantered away for the Wilton place.

He had a strangely powerful impulse to turn the head of the horse on the out trail and leave Clayrock and its evil crime behind him forever. Curiously enough, it was not the thought of Beatrice Wilton that stopped him now, but the knowledge that Peter Lang was yonder in the garden of the house, using his wits to solve this mystery.

So Sherry held on his way to the Wilton house, and walked his horse up the steep carriage road to the stable. The Chinese cook came out from the kitchen with a tin of scraps in his hand, stared at Sherry with fear and wonder, as at a dangerous being from a strange world. Tiny Lew went around to the front of the house and there he found the sheriff, Lang, and Doctor Layman all gathered in a close group discussing some clothes which lay on the ground before them.

Lang had discovered them among the trees, by closely following up the trail of Fennel, where it left the spot where Wilton had fallen. They consisted of the overcoat, the old hat, and the clumsy boots of Fennel, which he had worn when he confronted the three a little earlier on this tragic day.

"Murderers run, of course, after they've done the killing," said the doctor. "I suppose there isn't any doubt that Fennel is the man who did this thing?"

"It looks that way, of course," said the sheriff.

"Thank goodness, he can't go far!" said Layman. "Not with his build and his face! He'd made himself well enough known around Clayrock, and in a few hours you'll have him, sheriff!"

Here Lang put in: "There's somebody else to be considered in this job!"

Sherry glared at him. And when he failed to catch the eye of his friend he said roughly: "What d'you mean by that, Pete?"

Pete Lang waved off the question.

"I'll talk to the sheriff," he persisted. "Murder's a black thing, and if there's any way of getting to the truth about it, I want to help."

"Aye," said Herbert Moon in his soft voice, "murder is black! But in this part of the world there are too many who don't agree with your viewpoint, I'm afraid. Murder is black! And there's always night gathered around it. Can you help us out of the dark, Mr. Lang?"

"I can," said Pete Lang. "I want to tell you what I've seen Miss Wilton do."

"Pete!" cried Sherry in agony.

"Man! Man!" protested the doctor. "Beatrice! Beatrice Wilton? What are you talking about?"

"I think you know your duty, Lang," was all the sheriff remarked.

"I know my duty. I'm gunna do it. I got a clear case. I'm gunna state it! Me and old Tiny, yonder, seen this here girl practicing off in the woods with a small-caliber revolver with a silencer on it, so that you didn't hear any explosion. You just heard a sort of puff. Well, a while back Tiny ran into her in the woods sitting pretty thoughtful, and that gun in her lap. And now I want to point out that Wilton was killed wiht a bullet out of just such a gun, and that him and me, follering close on behind, didn't hear any sound of a gun!"

"It was the wind!" exclaimed Sherry eagerly. "The wind was howling and roaring through the trees, just then. There was enough wind to kill the sound."

"The sound of a revolver—not more'n forty yards away!" persisted Lang.

Sherry groaned. He saw the absurdity of such a claim as he had just made.

The doctor and the sheriff said nothing. They watched and listened intensely, their eyes never stirring from the face of Lang, who continued: "It ain't easy to say these things. I gotta explain that I hate sneaking murder. And a woman that shoots to kill is a lot more sneaking than a man, because she's got a lot more chances of getting off, if she's caught. Well, this one is caught, and I hope she hangs for it—and the prettier her face, the more I hope that she hangs! After we started hunting for Wilton—missing him on the path

88

—we heard a sound in the woods. I asked Tiny Lew to go after it. He did, and he found this here girl crouching in a bush. There was a gun in her hand.

"The barrel of that gun was still warm. There was an empty shell in the cylinder. The girl was scared to death. The first thing she said was: 'I didn't do it!' Sherry had to carry her back to the place of the killing. She pretty near fainted. And—there was blood on her hand!"

So, rapidly, heaping up the important facts, one on another, Pete Lang made out the case against the girl.

The sheriff joined his small hands together and, raising his head, looked up at the dark flight of the clouds across the sky.

Then Doctor Layman exclaimed bitterly: "Moon, you're not going to take this thing seriously? You don't mean to say that you'll register all this against Beatrice Wilton?"

The sheriff did not answer.

"Great Scott, man!" cried Layman. "Don't you know Beatrice Wilton? A lady if ever one—"

"A Wilton," said the sheriff. "I know that she's a Wilton. And they have a strange sort of a record, Doctor Layman."

"Whose voice have you against her?" asked the doctor, who seemed in an odd state of fear and excitement. "That man's! An unknown cowpuncher! A gun fighter—proved by the fact that Wilton hired him for that purpose. He testifies against Beatrice Wilton! Sheriff, may he not have some reason for wanting to put the blame on other shoulders? Doesn't it stand to reason that unless he had some such purpose, he never would have accused her? A Western man doesn't go out of his way, as he has done, to accuse a woman against whom he could not possibly have any grudge."

The sheriff looked mildly upon the doctor and appeared to be considering this statement, while Lang raised a finger and pointed it like a gun at the speaker.

"You're talking a lot and you're talking loud!" he cautioned.

"Do you think that I care a whit for your threats?" demanded the doctor, actually taking a step nearer to Lang. "I dsepise you and all the rest of your gun-fighting crew? Sheriff, I want you to tell me right now that you're going to discount the testimony of this ruffian!"

The sheriff merely said: "Mr. Sherry was with Lang. You were with him at the time the shooting must have taken place, Sherry?"

"I was," said Sherry gloomily.

"Have you any reason to suspect that Lang is twisting the truth?" persisted the sheriff.

Sherry stared at the face of his friend.

"It's all right, Lew," said Lang gently. "You don't have to stick by me in this. I know just how you feel!"

Sherry groaned aloud.

"I can't turn a lie against Pete," he confessed. "Lord forgive me—but I got to say that everything he's said is correct. He hasn't exaggerated a single thing."

"I'm sorry to hear it," said the sheriff. "It makes it necessary for me to see Miss Wilton. Will you tell me where she is?"

The doctor threw up both hands to the sky, and letting them fall again, he struck one against his forehead heavily.

"She's in that room to the right. The one with the French door opening on the garden."

"Will you come with me?" asked the sheriff of Tiny Lew.

The big man followed little Herbert Moon to the indicated door. They tapped.

"Who's there?" called the uncertain voice of the girl.

"Sheriff Moon," said the man of the law.

There was a frightened gasp inside.

And Sherry, interpreting that stifled cry with blinding suddenness, gave his shoulder to the door and burts it open, with a shivering and crashing of broken glass. He, lurching into the chamber, saw Beatrice Wilton running to the center table. Her hand had scooped up the revolver which lay there and raised it toward her own head when the reaching hand of Sherry struck at her.

The weight of the blow flung her against the wall; and the gun exploded with its ominous, soft noise and thudded a bullet into the ceiling, while Sherry, leaping on, gathered the girl safely into his arms.

CHAPTER SEVENTEEN

FOLLOWING SWIFTLY on the choked noise of the shot, Lang and the doctor would have rushed into the room, but the sheriff turned toward them and waved them away.

"It's my duty to examine Miss Wilton," he said. "Mr. Sherry is already here. He'll serve me as a witness. If you gentlemen wish to assist me, you may search the grounds again. Doctor Layman, perhaps you'll inform the coroner?"

With that he closed the broken door in their faces and turned back to the room.

Beatrice Wilton had sunk into a chair. Leaning to one side, supporting herself with one stiffened arm, while her head hung low, she looked about to faint. Sherry stood behind her, his arms folded. He needed that stricture of his big, hard, arm muscles across his breast; otherwise, he felt as though his heart would tear its way out of his breast.

The sheriff took a chair by the center table. He waved to Sherry to take another, but Sherry shook his head.

"Miss Wilton," said the sheriff, "you are under arrest for the death of Oliver Wilton. Whatever you say now may be used against you in a court of law as admissible testimony. Nothing will be forced from you.

You are fully warned about the danger of talking?"

She swayed a little. So much so, that Sherry put down a hand as if prepared to steady her. But then she straightened herself and looked slowly around the room, as though she wished to gain strength and courage from familiar sights. Sherry, with an aching heart, followed that glance. It was a dainty place, thoroughly feminine. There was an Italian bed, low, with a gilt back; and before the bed a painted screen which almost obscured it, so that the chamber could serve as a living room. All was bright and cheerful, gay little landscapes on the wall, and three rugs blurring the floor with color. But the broken door seemed to Sherry to have a strange meaning; so had the security of this girl been lost, and the danger of the world been let in upon her!

Now she looked back at the sheriff and nodded slowly.

"I understand," said she.

Her voice was steady, and the heart of Sherry leaped again—with admiration, this time. And he told himself, bitterly, that he cared little what she had done. She was beautiful, and she was brave. That, in itself, was enough for him.

"You know that I don't want to take advantage of you?" went on Herbert Moon. "For that matter, your friend Sherry wouldn't let me, I suppose!"

She looked hastily over her shoulder at the towering form and the frowning brow of Tiny Lew.

"You didn't know he is your friend?" went on Moon.

And she, still glancing up, smiled faintly at Sherry —an incredulous smile, he thought.

"What I want you to do," said the sheriff, "is to talk freely. Times like this unlock the heart. They break down the barrier which we ordinarily erect against the eye and the ear of the world. Well, the more freely you talk now, the easier it will be to establish your innocence. We have certain facts against you. I'm not allowed to tell you what they are. I even should not tell you that a statement by a suspected person immediately after arrest usually bears with double force in the eyes of the law. In this time of excitement and confusion, truth is supposed to be nearer to the tongue of the one under arrest. You have something to say, of course. Will you say it to me now?"

Sherry broke in: "Why should she talk now? This is a case where she ought to have a lawyer. If I were she, I wouldn't say a word to anybody without the advice of a lawyer, and a good one!"

"That is usually a good rule," said the sheriff. "I'm sorry to say that a great many officers of the law are only interested in securing convictions. But I have grown old in my work, Mr. Sherry, and I hope you'll believe me when I say that I have only one great wish in every case—and that is to secure justice, not prison stripes, for the accused. Now, Miss Wilton, will you talk to me?"

Sherry suddenly left his post back of her chair and stood beside the sheriff, facing her. At that, her eyes no longer wandered. She spoke to the sheriff, but her eyes, all the while, were fixed upon the handsome, stern face of Sherry. And sometimes she looked down to his big hands, sun-blackened; and sometimes her glance swept across the great breadth of his shoulders— famous shoulders were they, up and down the length of the range.

She said:

"I was walking in the woods. I was disturbed—" She paused.

"I was afraid," she murmured.

"You were afraid," said the sheriff, encouraging her gently. "Will you tell me of what you were afraid?"

She moistened her lips, tried to speak, hesitated. And then, looking earnestly upon Sherry, as though she were drawing strength and inspiration from him, she continued: "I was afraid of my uncle."

Sherry raised a warning hand.

"I wouldn't interrupt her!" exclaimed Herbert Moon, with some asperity.

"Don't you see," broke in Sherry, "that if you admit

you were afraid of your uncle, you furnish with your own testimony a reason why you might have wished to—"

"To kill him?"

She spoke straight out, her voice perfectly steady. "I understand that, of course. I'm trying to tell the truth!"

"You were afraid of your uncle," said the sheriff. "You said that, as my friend here interrupted. Sherry, I'm afraid that I'll have to complete this interview without you .Will you step outside?"

Beatrice Wilton stiffened suddenly in the chair.

"No!" she exclaimed. "Please let him stay. He helps me to tell the truth!"

"Then—by all means," said the sheriff, as gentle as ever. "Let us continue this conversation, like three friends. And will you remember, my dear young girl, that it is always best to tell the whole truth—usually even to win in the law, and always, I trust, for the sake of the God who hears us all!"

Now there was not a great deal of religion on the cow range, and the stern men of the law were hardly apt to have sacred names upon their lips any more than the reckless cowpunchers and gunmen whom they tried to keep in order. Therefore, Sherry heard this speech with a little shock of surprise and of awe. And the girl looked for a moment from him and toward Herbert Moon. But instantly her glance came back to the big man.

"You were afraid of your uncle," went on the sheriff. "And why were you afraid of him?"

"My father's money was left in trust for one year. At the end of that time, it passes into the hands of my guardian. Uncle Oliver is my guardian. In a few more days, my money would all have been placed in his hands. But still I would have a claim on it. Now, suppose I died. Uncle Oliver would be the next heir. You understand?"

The sheriff nodded.

"Your uncle would have been the next heir. And

you thought that he was capable of—taking your life for the sake of that money?"

"I didn't know. But I was afraid!"

"What gave you such an idea?"

"There were a good many things. He had queer ways. He lived in the house like a general in a fort. He was always practicing with weapons in the woods behind the house. Besides, I once overheard—"

She paused.

However, the sheriff did not offer to encourage her, and it was Sherry who nodded slightly.

Then she went on, speaking directly to him: "It has been a rather lonely house to live in—since my father's death. I don't know why. It used to seem very cheerful, before. It was like living at the top of a wave. One could look down all over the town, and the plain, and the hills and the mountains beyond. But afterwards, it seemed cold and dark. I was always lonely. I used to hate the house and spend a good deal of my time in the garden or walking among the trees. And one day I was out very late. I should have been home before. It was really after sunset. Yes, I remember that I could see patches of red sky in the west, between the tree trunks. I was coming in slowly, even late as it was, because I hated to reach the house, and because I went slowly, I supose I made little noise. Then I came on the sound of voices. I heard my uncle talking excitedly."

"And who was the other man?" asked the sheriff.

"I don't know. He spoke more softly. I hardly made out a word he said. It sounded a little like the voice of Doctor Layman, however."

'Will you go on then?"

"I heard my uncle cry out: 'I tell you that I haven't them. I've lost them. I haven't a single one!' Then he swore, like a man frantic with excitement, and he went on: 'Do you suppose that if I were able to find them, and have them, I'd waste my perfectly good time here trying to—' "

"How did he finish that sentence?"

"He didn't finish it. But then he said: 'Heaven for-

95

give me! Heaven forgive me! People think I'm an honorable man. If they knew what I had in mind and heart—and then you come here to badger me! But I swear that I haven't one of them. Would I be staying here if I did have them?'

"After that I clearly heard the other man say: 'That's your responsibility. You have had them. They were in your charge. You ought to know that you'll have to make good for them. You ought to be able to lay your hands on enough money to make a part payment. That's not asking a great deal!'

"My uncle answered, excited as ever, but a wind began to rise, and I couldn't hear any more. I went on back to the house. And ever since that moment, I've been sick with fear of him. I've never known when I'd die in my sleep. I've feared even the food on the table before me!"

"Very well. And then today?"

"I used to go out with a revolver, practicing. I thought that I should learn to take care of myself, you see. Today, I was in the garden, doing that. I'd filled my revolver and fired one shot—at a sapling."

"Did you hit it?"

She blinked

"No—I think not. I walked on through the trees and came out onto a path—and saw a man lying face down! I leaned over him. I saw it was Uncle Oliver. I touched his face to try to rouse him. My hand came away sticky with blood! Then I went mad with fear and ran off into the brush; and you found me there—and brought me back!"

She smiled, a twisted smile, at Sherry; and then closed her eyes and turned white.

CHAPTER EIGHTEEN

AT THIS moment it appeared to Sherry that the poor girl had proved her case completely, and he stepped a little forward so that he could turn and look more fully into the face of the sheriff, for he wanted to see the conviction appear in the eyes of that man of the law. But he only saw the sheriff lean forward with a peculiar keenness of expression, and instead of using gentle words, or none, when the girl was so overwhelmed, Sheriff Moon said quickly: "Of couse, it isn't a pleasant thing to see a dead man. It's not pleasant a bit. That unnerved you. That sent you off scampering through the brush. I suppose that your brain spun and turned dark, didn't it? Poor girl!"

"Yes, yes!" she muttered, without opening her eyes.

Comforting enough the words of the sheriff had been, except that they had called up the grisly picture of the dead too vividly, but in sound and manner they were not so kind—they had come out rapidly, with a sort of savage eagerness, which Sherry was at a loss to account for.

He said to himself: 'There's poison in that little man. There's poison in all little men!' For often it seemed to him that the smaller the man, the more waspish the temper. For his own part, anger advanced upon him slowly. He could endure many taunts and many insults, but only by degrees passion inflamed his brain, until at last he could not endure, and had to fight. So he felt now that the sheriff had allowed bitterness to master him and had struck at a helpless girl.

Her eyes opened again, and she was looking at him, her eyes very wide, but little seeing in them.

The sheriff stood up.

"I won't bother you any longer," he said. "You've made your statement as complete as you care to have it, I suppose?"

"I don't think of anything else," she said.

"I'm going outside," said the sheriff. "But Mr. Sherry will stay in here with you, in case you want anything, or if you feel faint. Mr. Sherry will take care of you!"

He went out with a brisk step, and all at once she roused herself out of her trance and sprang up and ran to Tiny Lew. She looked very small. She did not come up to his shoulder, and she caught with her hands at his arms, hard and stiff as the large steel cables which made a ship's crew, stowing them below in ample circles, curse.

"He doesn't believe in me," said Beatrice Wilton.

"He's a fool if he doesn't!" exclaimed Sherry from his heart. "But he didn't say that he didn't believe. You take these fellows of the law and they're great on not committing themselves."

"He doesn't believe in me!" she repeated, shaking her head, as though she were casting off the importance of Sherry's faint denial. "Tell me! He doesn't believe what I said?"

"They're queer—all these man hunters!" he told her. "It don't matter what he thinks, though. He's not the judge. And he's a long way from being twelve men on the jury."

At this, the strength of her frenzy of fear relaxed a good deal; she was faint, rather than frantic, once more; and she dropped into a chair by the table, locked her hands together, and stared at him over them.

Sherry was fascinated, for it had been many years since he had lived in the land where women's hands are white and slender soft. He almost had forgotten that there are hands which have not been thickened, and spread, and blunted by pulling at the reins, or by swinging axes; hands not reddened from work in dishwater, or in washing suds on Mondays; hands not roughened from scrubbing with sand soap, from dragging heavy brooms across splintered floors.

But she was out of the other world, delicately and softly made, and so Sherry stared at those two hands which gripped and fought at one another until they trembled. The wrists were like the hands. No bulging cords stared from them. He could have held them both easily in the grip of one hand; but the more he felt the excess of his power over her the more he was subdued by two intense emotions—a vast pity for her, vast awe because of the delicate cunning with which nature had made her.

When she spoken again, her voice had changed. She was hoarse, as though she had been screaming into a wind, or sobbing heavily for a long time.

"Do you think he'll bring me up for trial? Do you think that, Mr. Sherry?"

"That's not for him to say," he told her. "That's for the coroner's jury to say."

She held out both hands to him, palms up; her eyes were half closed and he had a shuddering fear that she was about to weep.

"Don't you understand?" she asked. "Everybody in this place does just as Sheriff Moon wants. He does the thinking for all of Clayrock. They would think nothing of accusing me, if he so much as frowned at me. They would think nothing of—of—"

She could not say the word, but she clasped her hands and laid one of them against her throat. He saw that a fine blue vein ran up the right side of her neck; and it seemed to Sherry that he was looking through translucent white and seeing that vein, deeply hidden.

"Great Scott!" said Sherry. "What are you thinking of? Do you think that people would allow such a thing? Do you think that there are jail doors that would hold you? Do you think that there are not hands which would bring you safely out?"

He held such a hand out to her, not as one who calls attention to himself, but as a man speaking out of the heat of emotion which gathers him up as a strong draft gathers up a powerful flame. He was a magnificent man, this Lewis Sherry, not meant to be ironed out into a common background of stiff white shirt fronts, and black dinner jackets. Out of such a background little appears except grace, and cunning, stinging words; but Sherry looked at that moment like a glorious animal with hands as strong as metal, and with the divine mind all on fire for action.

She looked at him from foot to head, and suddenly she smiled at him.

"*You* would tear the doors open for me!" she said in the same husky voice.

Then as though she gathered strength from him, and from the thought, she lifted herself from the chair and came to him, still smiling. She stood just under him, so that she had to bend back her head a little to look up into his face, and a sad sense of sweetness, like the fragrance of late roses in the fall of the year, possessed Sherry. He wanted to ask her not to smile, her beauty and her nearness made his heart ache so with the knowledge that she trusted him so deeply, and that she was so near perishing.

"I'll never lose all heart again," she told him. "I see that you believe in me!"

"I do," said Sherry. "I believe in you!"

He could manage to make the words simple, but he could not take control of his voice, which rumbled out in a great organ peal, a declaration of faith. If he had said that he loved her, that he worshiped her, that he would serve her in all possible ways, it could not have been put more clearly than by all that his voice inferred. And she glowed beneath him. The weariness and the trouble that had marked her face disappeared, and out of her shone that light which joy kindles in a beautiful girl.

She was saying: "If you want to help me, go to Doctor Layman. If any one knows a way of doing things for me now, he is the man. Tell him that I asked you to go to him. And oh, if you wish to help me, follow what he says! For he's wiser than all the rest. He's even wiser than the sheriff—and so much kinder!"

He knew that he was close to some frantic declaration, and because he was ashamed to break out, and because, too, the mention of another man had somehow brought a soberer touch to him, he left her at once and stumbled out into the garden.

He was met by blinding light. During the brief time he had been in the room with the girl the wind had changed, and the dark cloud masses, no longer shooting south, were rolling toward the northeast in walls and towers between which the rich blue of the sky reached through. It was nearly sunset; the light was golden; hope suddenly filled the world—and also the heart of Lewis Sherry.

The sheriff had gone off to the town, and Sherry found the man he wanted pacing up and down through the garden, pausing now and then to kick at a stone, his head bent toward the earth.

"Beatrice Wilton told me to come to you," said Sherry. "She said that you would know what to tell me to do."

The doctor looked up at him by degrees; his hands were locked behind his back, which made his slender figure seem yet more spare, so that he looked to Sherry, at the moment, a very type of the intellectual—his physical existence was so dominated by that imposing brow.

"She sent you to me?" queried the doctor.

"Yes."

"The deuce she did!" murmured Layman.

He actually walked on, kicking the small stones out of his way as he went, and yet Sherry was not offended, for he told himself that it was the sheer excess of sorrow of mind that forced Layman to be rude.

At length, coming to the end of the path, the doctor turned upon him and said slowly: "She sent you to me.

Did she say what right you had to come to talk to me about her?"

"She said," quoted Sherry, "that you would know what I could do to help her."

"To help her? Does she need help?" asked the doctor in the same sharp way.

Sherry was a little irritated.

"After her talk with the sheriff," said he, "I think she does."

"The sheriff was stubborn, was he?" murmured Layman. "I believe he has the reputation. But she couldn't do anything with him?"

"Nothing but tell her story," said Sherry.

"And that did no good?"

"Not a bit—so far as I could see."

Then Sherry added: "Suppose I ask just why she sent me to you for orders?"

The doctor looked at him in doubt. Then he shrugged his shoulders.

"Suppose I say that we're engaged to be married. Would that make any further explanation necessary?"

CHAPTER NINETEEN

THE VAGUE hopes that had been rising in the mind of Sherry were rebuffed. As a strong wind will clear away mist suddenly, so the passion of Sherry was blown to tatters in an instant. Then, slowly, he settled himself to face the new problem.

"I don't mind saying that it makes a lot of difference," he said quietly.

"I thought so," said the doctor. "It takes a well-balanced youngster to see Beatrice a few times without losing his head."

He nodded at Sherry. It was really impossible to take offense at this bluntness on his part, for it was plain that he was partly thinking out loud, partly expressing a viewpoint to another. There was no malice in his manner. It was simply the expression of a calm conviction. So Sherry made no answer.

The doctor went on in his rather irritated manner:

"That may change your viewpoint altogether, as a matter of fact?"

"About helping her?" asked Sherry.

"Exactly."

"No," said Sherry, "it doesn't at all."

"Ha! I wonder!" said the doctor.

He began to pace up and down again, kicking in his half-abstracted and half-venomous way at the small stones in the path. He halted, with his back turned.

"No one can help her without pouring his whole heart into the job!"

"I suppose not," answered Sherry.

Layman swung about on him.

"You're free to go. You know that," he said. "You won't get the ten thousand that you were hired for."

Sherry did not reply to this. He wondered if the other was trying to torment him as a test of his temper and of his steadfastness.

"You're not going?" inquired Layman.

"No."

"In addition, there may be danger in staying about this place and trying to help Beatrice. Have you thought of that?"

"More sailors, do you mean?" asked Sherry.

"Ha?" exclaimed the doctor. Then he went on, thoughtfully: "You've looked a little way beneath the surface, at least!"

"Thank you," said Sherry, dryly.

"Don't be proud! Don't be proud!" said the doctor. "There will be plenty of time for you to show what you're made of before this little affair is over."

He laughed suddenly, and added: "I can assure you of that! Plenty of time, and plenty of ways!"

He went up to Sherry and gripped his arm with such force that the big man was surprised.

"You went down to the hotel. Did you find out anything about Fennel? Did you find out anything about the murderer?"

"I found out that he's pretty deep," said Sherry.

"In what way? What did you find out?"

"He posed as a drunkard. Matter of fact, he probably never touched a drop except in public."

"Ha?" said the doctor. "How could that be? I've said that he was a victim of alcoholic poisoning. Do you think that I imagined it, my friend?"

"Good-by," said Sherry.

"What?"

Sherry walked off, but Layman followed after him and touched his arm.

"You're right," he said, when the other turned again. "I have no right to take advantage of your generous attitude toward Beatrice—and me. But the fact is that I'm half mad. This thing has upset me, naturally. You see that, Sherry? As a matter of fact, I value your help hugely. It might make the difference of the turning of the scale."

"I hope so."

"So go on and tell me about the sailor—the pretended sailor—whatever he was. You say that he didn't drink?"

"I don't go against a doctor's word. I suppose you know your business."

"I'm not a genius of the profession," said Layman. "But I think I know alcoholism when I see it. It's not the rarest disease in this part of the world."

"Very well. I tell you only what I know. I've been in Fennel's room twice. I saw that more than a bottle of whiskey had been used up between visits. Well, that seemed incredible. A man with more than a quart of whiskey in him doesn't walk up a path and confront another as Fennel confronted Wilton a while ago—even allowing that he's a freak and can carry twice as much liquor as a normal man."

"More than a quart? Of course not! That's impossible for human nature, without making a man nearly senseless, I suppose."

"Very well. The liquor was gone. I looked about to find how it had vanished. And I saw a little trap set into the lead of the drainage pipe. I went down below. The ground was reeking with whiskey fumes. There you are. It's fairly clear that if Fennel drank enough to have alcoholic poisoning, he dodged a lot more by pouring the stuff down the pipe."

"What idiots," said Layman, "men can be! There's a fellow with murder planned, and incidentally he wanted to work up a great reputation as a drinker. And so the drainage pipe scheme. Well— And still there's no trace of Fennel! And the fool of a sheriff," he went on, "is trying to hang the guilt on the shoulders of Beatrice Wilton! Heaven forgive him for a blind man!"

"I don't see this—why should Fennel have killed Wilton?"

"Is that strange? He couldn't get what he wanted. Look at his clothes. Rags and tatters. And a beggar never gets enough. He wants nothing less than a fortune laid into his hands. So with our friend Fennel. He couldn't get what he wanted. So he used a gun."

"I don't see him using a gun with a silencer," said Sherry. "He didn't impress me as the type. A common 'fore-the-mast sailor would hardly go in for the niceties."

"You forget what the newspapers do for people these days," said the doctor bitterly. "They not only suggest crimes, but they also suggest safe ways of working them. If murders were never reported in the public prints, you'd find the lists cut down ten per cent in no time!"

"But there was Fennel," persisted Sherry, "not asking for a great deal. Apparently, all that he wanted was enough to keep drunk on. Wilton would have given him that much."

"Wilton was a stubborn fellow," said the doctor. "What makes you think that he would have given it?"

"Because he was almost frightened to death," said Sherry.

"Are you sure of that?"

"I walked down the path behind him. He hardly could keep himself in hand."

"Fennel a sham—Wilton frightened to death by a sham—hands pointing to Beatrice—great heaven," said Layman, "who can see through this muddle?"

They were interrupted by the arrival of the sheriff, the coroner, and the coroner's jury, who had been hastily gathered. They were brought into the living room of the Wilton house, where the murdered man had been placed on a couch. He looked very pale and peaceful to Sherry, with the smile of death on his lips. And yet that death seemed more horrible than usual in such a place, for all the process of a normal life was scattered about—a newspaper here, a book, open and face down, there. The disarray of the chair, the rumpled corner of a rug, all seemed to make it impossible to believe that Oliver Wilton lay dead.

The coroner was a fat man whose wind was quite gone. He dropped into a chair and fanned himself with his hat.

"Pretty neat room, ain't it?" said he. "I never been here before. You, Pat?"

Pat admitted that it was his first visit.

"That's the trouble with a lot of these rich swells," declared the coroner. "They're above the common people. They got no time for them. And the first thing that they know, they trip up their heels, and they got to have just as much law around as the next man!"

There was general agreement with this statement.

Then the coroner ordered the room to be cleared except for the clerk, the sheriff, and the first witness, who was to be Doctor Layman.

Back to the garden went Sherry and Pete Lang. And the face of Pete was serene and happy.

Sherry said to him quietly: "I suppose you're heading back for the range, Pete?"

"And why?" asked Pete.

"Because you're through here, as far as I can make out."

"And how do you make it out, son? Will you tell me that?"

"Your boss is dead, Pete. There's no more money here for you."

"Then I'll be a dog-gone philanthropist," said Lang, "and work on just for sheer patroitism, as you might call it."

"To hang a girl if you can?" asked Sherry coldly.

"That rides you, partner, don't it?" asked Pete.

Sherry was silent, and Lang looked calmly upon the stern face of his friend.

"I'm gunna work, and work," said he. "I never felt more at home than I do right now. The law can do what it wants, but I got an idea that Pete Lang is the one that's gunna prove the case!"

"What makes you think that?"

"Lemme ask you—what become of the letter that Wilton received from Fennel?"

"I forget about that. It must be in his coat pocket. I remember that he put it there!"

"I remembered, too. And here it is!"

He spread it out in the hand of Sherry, and the letter read:

Dear Skipper: So that we can cut the buisness short, suppose that you cum along with some of the pearls? I don't ask for much. Just say that you bring along a handful, and not of the smallest. That wood hold me. I don't want to rob you. I just want my shair.

Respectfully,
Fennel

107

"But he didn't bring the pearls," said Sherry, "and so he was murdered."

"Didn't he bring them? What do you think of this?" asked Pete calmly.

And, scooping a hand into his pocket, he brought it out with the palm well filled with the milky luster of a heap of pearls!

CHAPTER TWENTY

OVER THESE jewels they bowed their heads. They were by no means of uniform size, shape, or quality; but some were like small pears, and others were irregular globes, and others, again were what are called *perle boutons* by jewelers, that is to say flat on the bottom, and formed like hemispheres. There were very small pearls, and there was one pear-shaped jewel of considerable size.

"You're going to show those to the coroner and his jury?" asked Sherry.

"Of course," said Lang. "These and the letter. They're testimony, ain't they?"

"You're not going to show them," declared Sherry firmly.

"And why not, Tiny? Is there anything else in the case that argues as much as this?"

"And what does it argue?" asked Sherry.

"That Fennel never killed Wilton."

"How do you make that out?"

"That's a simple trick. Look here. Fennel writes to Wilton. 'Bring me down a flock of pearls,' says he. Wilton does it. Still, Fennel shoots him? Why, I ask you? It ain't reasonable and it ain't likely. A gent holds up Wilton. Wilton comes through with the goods. At least, he takes down the stuff that's asked for. He wouldn't 've done that if he hadn't intended to pass them over."

"And then?"

"Then what happened is easy to guess. The girl, all worked up about things, comes through the woods, sees Wilton, and takes a crack at him. He drops on his face. Fennel, scared to death, figures that his turn is coming next—maybe that the bullet really was meant for him. He beats it into the trees."

"Why should he chuck off hat and shoes and coat?"

"Why not? He wants to make tracks as fast as he can go. As he goes whisking through the brush his hat is knocked off. He can't make time in that long over-coat—you remember that it pretty near dragged the ground?—so he throws that off. And still his shoes are in his way. Look at the size of those shoes. Twelves, I'd say! Well, he chucks those shoes off, too, and goes on barefooted!"

"Through that rough going?"

"What's rough going to a sailor that's hardened up his feet using them bare to go aloft on iron-hard cordage?"

Sherry, stumped and disgusted with this perfect logic, still struggled.

"Look at it another way," he suggested. "They walk down the path together, Fennel and Wilton. Fennel wants to see the goods, and Wilton shows him the pearls. Fennel says they're not enough. That's the point, perhaps, where they stop and argue. You remember?"

"Yes."

"Wilton insists that's all he'll give to Fennel. Fennel gets angry. Finally he pulls a gun and shoots Wilton down, in a blind rage."

"And goes on without taking the pearls which he's just seen Wilton, by your account, drop back into his coat pocket?"

"Yes, because he's too frightened by what he's done."

109

"Tell me straight, Sherry. Was Fennel the sort of a fellow who would be easily scared?"

Sherry bit his lip. Certainly Fennel had appeared to be a man who had plenty of nerve.

"Half a second to lean over and drag out this stuff. Was Fennel the fellow to overlook such a sure bet as that?" went on Lang, triumphant in his progress toward the truth.

Then he summed up: "Fennel couldn't have been shown those pearls, if he committed the murder. And he wouldn't have shot unless he'd had a chance to see them. And once having seen them, he would of taken them along when he bolted."

"Maybe the pearls were only a dodge with him," suggested Sherry. "Perhaps he only wanted to use the pearls as a snare to trap Wilton and get him out into the garden?"

"You can fit in a 'perhaps' to pretty near anything," said Lang; "but I tell you this, old son, when I finish telling my yarn to the coroner and his jury, I'll lay the long odds that they put the girl in jail charged with murder in the first degree."

"And that," said Sherry, "is what you're not going to do."

"Hello!" cried Lang. "And why not?"

"She's got to have a fair chance," said Sherry. "You can't stack the cards against her."

"Stack the cards? I'm not pulling any tricks against her. What have I got against the girl?"

"You hate them all—everything in skirts," said Sherry. "Isn't that true?"

"I see through them," answered Lang. "They've smashed my life. They've double-crossed me every turn!"

"But here's one case where you're going to talk soft and be nice," said Sherry.

"Are you as hard hit as that?" asked his friend.

"I am."

"You want me to hold out this stuff?"

"I do."

110

Lang groaned.

"Don't you see, man," he urged, "that the girl's a cold-blooded little piece? She's too pretty to be good, in the first place!"

"She's got a hard enough row to hoe now," answered Sherry. "When the sheriff and I broke into her room, she tried to shoot herself. That's about enough to finish her, I suppose, when the sheriff gets through talking. I ask you again—will you give her a chance, man?"

At this, Pete Lang struck a hand against his forehead.

"Here's my only pal," said he, "comes to me and says: 'Pete, old man, for the sake of old times, will you gimme a chance to tie a rope around my neck and hang myself from your front door?' What am I to say? Boy, boy, you'd never get nothing out of her except a big laugh when she was in the clear!"

"You may be right," said Sherry.

"What do you think yourself about her?"

"Lord knows!"

"Tiny, you think that she's guilty!"

"I do," groaned Sherry.

"But you'd carry on?"

"I love her," said Sherry, with a sad simplicity.

Lang rolled a cigarette with fumbling fingers.

"You love her," he said. "You gotta chuck yourself away for her! By grab, it's always that way. The straight gents love the poison!"

He lighted his cigarette, and through swirling smoke his tormented eyes stared at his friend.

Sherry held out his hand and waited, and finally Lang made a convulsive gesture, of last argument.

"They'll jail her and try her, without this," he said. "But with this handful of stuff, they'll hang her. Without it they won't I should say. They'll only hang a doubt on her that'll disgrace her all her life, until a poor sucker like you comes along and marries her—and gets his throat cut a couple of months later."

The hand of Sherry still waited in mid-air, and at last Lang clutched and shook it with vigor.

"I'm wrong," he said, "I'm turning loose another plague on the world, and all because it wears a pretty face! Lord forgive me for the damage that she's gunna do!"

"We've got plenty of other things to do around here," said Sherry. "We want to run down the whole secret life of this Oliver Wilton. It may be that we'll learn enough to clear her altogether. You're fighting on my side now, Pete?"

"But mind you, son," he cautioned gravely, "the best thing that we can do is to turn in our evidence straight, and then pack and ride for the range. We never have had any luck in Clayrock. We're never going to have any luck. And there you are! It's my hunch. I've given you a fair warning."

To this Sherry made no answer, for the door opened, and he was summoned in before the coroner to give his testimony.

They were gloomy, stern faces, these twelve men. One might have thought they that had eaten something extremely bitter to the taste, so were their mouths puckered and awry.

The coroner was no stickler for form or legalities. He said directly: "Things look bad for the girl, Sherry. Now, what you gotta say about her at the murder?"

Sherry looked slowly around the room.

"Nothing," he answered at last.

At this, the sheriff rose from his chair.

"You've said things in my presence, Sherry. I want you to say them again. It's your duty."

"My duty?" said Sherry. "My duty to help toward the hanging of a girl I know is innocent?"

He said that in such a ringing voice that the jury started of one accord, and the fat coroner so hastily clapped his spectacles upon his nose that they dropped off a once before he could examine Sherry carefully.

"What you think," said the coroner, "ain't specially interesting just here and now, Sherry. We think that you're a straight shooter—both ways of using the word. Now we want to know what you seen and heard and

112

did today, about the time that Wilton was murdered. And though I take a lot of interest in a gent that's willing to help a poor girl, still, justice has gotta have its chance in the game. I ask you, man to man, will you talk out?"

Sherry raised a finger at them.

"I can tell you what I saw and heard," said he, "but I can't tell you what I felt. And that's what counts. And every man of you that has a wife, and every man of you that has a daughter, knows what I mean."

"That's not testimony," said the sheriff.

"The coroner runs this court, I believe, and not the sheriff," said Sherry icily.

"My dear lad," said the quiet voice of Moon, "we have our own way of fulfilling the law in this county, but we know testimony when we hear it. We don't want your opinions. We want your facts."

"To hound Beatrice Wilton!" exclaimed Sherry, black rage swallowing his judgment. He stepped forward toward the sheriff. "But if you're loading the dice against her," said he, "I want you to know that there are those who will stop your game."

"Hold on, young man!" exclaimed the coroner.

The jury gazed at the audacious Sherry with frightened eyes. For twenty-five years the sheriff had played a something more than human role in that community.

"He's young," said Herbert Moon as gently as ever. "He's young and he has a heart—a big heart, and a hot one. I hold nothing against him, but I think you'll get nothing worth while out of the testimony of Sherry, coroner."

"It looks like you're right," agreed the coroner. "Sherry, are you gunna talk, or do we have to bind you over for contempt—is that the right word, sheriff?"

"If you think that you need more testimony—yes," said the sheriff. "I suppose that we can hold him until he'll talk."

"If we need more?" muttered the coroner. "Well, we'll try Pete Lang, next. Sherry, we're finished with you, for a while."

So Sherry walked from the room, and found the doctor walking up and down the hall outside. He cast a bitter eye upon Sherry as Lang was called in to play his part of witness."

"You meant well, Sherry," said he, "but do you think that holding back in this fashion will be of any real use to Beatrice? They'll all guess blacker things than you could have said about her actions!"

Sherry did not answer. He felt that he had played a foolish part. This was a riddle which wits could not solve. But perhaps main force of hand could serve his purpose. So he looked darkly upon Layman and said nothing.

CHAPTER TWENTY-ONE

THE TESTIMONY of Lang was as disappointing as that of Sherry. He did not refuse to talk, but he refused to say anything of importance. "I don't know," was his invariable answer when he seemed to have been crowded into a corner, and at last the coroner said to the jury: "You boys can see for yourself. Lang won't talk; he's an old bunkie of Sherry's!"

They dismissed Lang.

The witnesses were not allowed to be present at the pronouncing of the verdict, but through the door the voice of the foreman was plainly heard declaring that in the estimation of twelve citizens of that jury, Beatrice Wilton was guilty of murder by shooting Oliver Wilton with "Exhibit A," which was the girl's own revolver, displayed upon a table in front of the coroner, together with the cast-off clothes of Fennel, and other items of interest in the case. She would be held in the Clayrock jail for trial.

But, the verdict having been given, the prisoner surrendered to the sheriff, Sherry and Lang were admitted to the room again. They found all the men in the room wearing long faces, unwilling to look at one another, with the exception of the sheriff, whose expression never varied, it seemed. A cheerful quiet always possessed his eye, and he looked as brightly and calmly upon Sherry and Lang and the girl as upon any of the jurors.

The latter were anxious to leave, but the sheriff would not let them go at once.

In the meantime, Beatrice Wilton sat by the window, utterly different from what she had been before. Sherry had dreaded facing her; he had expected that the strain would have broken down her nerve strength entirely and left her a wreck; but instead, she appeared perfectly calm and self-possessed. She and the sheriff alone had themselves under perfect control, while Layman went up to her, with Sherry and Lang as a sort of rear guard.

Layman sat down beside her and took her hand.

"Beatrice," he said, "it's going to be a long, hard fight!"

She looked at him without answering word or gesture; and her quiet manner staggered Sherry. If she had strength enough for this, she had strength enough for anything, he told himself—strength enough, say, for the slaying of a man! And once more the overwhelming surety of her guilt possessed his mind.

But there were compensating facts, if only they could be known; and he would know them, if there were strength in him, and wit in Lang, to unravel the skein of mystery.

Layman went on: "We'll need every penny we can put our hands on."

"You can sell some stock for me, Eustace," she replied.

"As soon as you give me power of attorney, and full rights to act for you, of course."

"Yes, naturally."

But here Lang put in: "We ain't hired men, ma'am, but we're volunteers. If we could have a chance to look through that house when we want to, it might be that we could turn up some things that would be useful to you."

"My dear Lang," said the doctor blankly, "what on earth could you discover in the house?"

"Enough, maybe, to save Miss Wilton," replied the puncher.

"Lang," began the doctor, "of course I know that you have the best will in the world, but—"

Beatrice Wilton leaned forward a little and raised a hand to silence Layman.

"You already know something," said she. "I'm sure that you know something that the coroner hasn't heard, Pete?"

She let that familiar name fall with such a gentle intonation that Sherry saw his hardy friend start a little; and he smiled in dour understanding.

But to this question Layman interposed: "My dear Beatrice, don't you see that it's going to make everything more difficult for me if I have to divide my time between the house and—"

"And the jail?" she finished for him, undisturbed.

Even Layman, cool as ice ordinarily, now flushed a little.

"I can't very well be in two places at once," he complained.

"Of course you can't. So let Lew Sherry and Pete Lang stay in the house."

"There's every reason against it," urged Layman. "These are known men, Beatrice."

"Known?" she echoed, raising her brows a little.

"I don't want to insult them. It's no insult to say they're known to have come here as guards to your uncle!"

"But what has that to do with me?"

"Don't you see? You'd have them up on the hill like a sort of standing army, ready to rush down and smash

116

the jail open, say, in case the trial went against you. Isn't that obvious? People know Sherry, particularly. He has a long and—efficient—record behind him. You understand, Beatrice, that from the very first, you must try to win public opinion to your side of the case! And you can't do that when you have two aces up your sleeve—and everybody knows about them! It's really very important. You ought to see that, dear."

"I didn't dream that it could mean so much," said she. "Of course, if that's the way of it, we'll just have to close the house."

"Naturally," said Layman. "Great Scott, what a blunder to have posted them up there like a pair of trained eagles on a crag! If you win, you win; if you lose the case, the pair of them come and split open the jail and take you out!"

Sherry could see the point of the argument clearly enough, but Lang persisted with much solemnity. He leaned a little closer to the girl and said slowly: "I think that I might turn up something worth while at the house. Serious and sober, ma'am, I'd like to try."

She looked earnestly at the puncher. Then: "Well, Eustace?" she asked.

The doctor hesitated. He looked at the girl rather than at Lang.

"Lang is a keen fellow," he said suddenly. "If he has an idea, let him try his best, of course. We can't afford to turn down any chances, no matter how small."

"That's settled, then, and the two of you will be there?"

She looked to Sherry and he, in turn, bowed his great, heavy bulk above her chair.

"You have small chances, anyway," said he, "and never a better chance than right now."

She looked fixedly up at him, not frightened, but thoughtful, considering; and again his judgment said to him, "Guilty!" and again his heart leaped and reveled in her beauty, and drove him on.

'What chance?" she asked him.

"Here are three of us," he replied. "I can answer

117

for Pete. If Layman hasn't a gun, I can lend him an extra Colt. The coroner is a fossil. The jury has not more than two fighting men in the whole outfit. We're not more than six steps from the door. Get up from your chair and walk straight for the door. You'll be halfway there before anyone challenges you. Then run. We'll cover your going and pile out behind you—"

"The sheriff?" she said.

"If Moon draws a gun," said Sherry through his teeth, "Heaven help him!"

"Eustace!" whispered the girl.

Layman, his face white, but his eyes very bright, listened, and said not a word. Lang dropped a hand upon the massive shoulder of his friend. It was his silent consent.

"It's your one real chance," said Sherry. "Do you understand me? For life!"

"Where could we go?"

"I'll find a place to take you. Lang and the doctor and I will take care of you."

"Sherry and Lang!" called the sheriff.

"He suspects something. Now is your time!" said Sherry.

"You mean it?"

"Yes, yes. But quickly!"

Suddenly, color leaped into her face.

"Not one step!" said the girl. "Why—it would be ruin for you, all three."

"Sherry!" said the sheriff.

Sherry turned heavily away and Herbert Moon went halfway across the room to meet him.

"I love a brave man," said the sherff, "but, my dear young fellow, even courage shouldn't attempt to move mountains!"

CHAPTER TWENTY-TWO

THE TOWN of Clayrock was filled for the trial days before it was due to be called. The town was put on the map, in a way, and the three hotels did big business. Prices for all things rose.

In the first place, there were the reporters who swarmed in. Newspapers in these days have to have their thrills to give hungry readers, and what is there better for this purpose than the case of a young and beautiful girl accused of murder? To make it better still, suppose the girl to be well raised, well educated, of good family! To cap the climax make the victim a blood relation—her father's own brother!

It was all that the newspapers could wish for, and they sent their reporters on long before the trial to work up the ground.

They found something to work. In the first place, there was the question, still wide open: "Did Fennel perform the murder, or is Beatrice Wilton guilty?"

Of course, the papers took sides. To some Beatrice Wilton was plainly guilty and the reporters almost said so. The man Fennel was an elusive shadow. He was hardly to be called a man; certainly, he had disappeared from Clayrock with as much thoroughness as though the wind had blown him through the town to be dissolved in air. So one faction seemed to doubt that Fennel ever existed. His battered shoes, his ragged overcoat—still whiskey-tainted according to some—and his old hat, were in evidence, of course, but they were discounted heavily. He had no motives. His past was unknown. His relations with Oliver Wilton were yet

119

to be established. In the meantime, here was Beatrice Wilton, young and beautiful, to be sure. But when has beauty not meant trouble? And behind her lay the dark background of the Wilton family. Into the dim past, they traced its sources. They listed down upon the account a blockade runner in the Civil War; a pair of brothers who had joined the forty-niners and only one of whom had come home, well-to-do, but streaked with silver scars. They followed the Wiltons into older days still. There was a Wilton-Durham feud in the first part of the nineteenth century. Some said that three had been killed. Some said thirty. There had been duels, too—there was a story of a Wilton who had fought with an enemy across a dining-room table, the muzzles of their outstretched pistols overlapping. And in the times of swords, still one found that the Wiltons had been involved in voilence!

Then, what more natural than that this "proud, keen, vigorous, fearless girl" should have taken her affairs into her own hands? She wanted possession of her own fortune. She did not want it to pass into the hands of her uncle even for a moment. That was motive sufficient—for a Wilton!

So the newspapers of the hostile faction printed photographs of Beatrice that showed her unsmiling, straight-eyed, keen as any man.

To the other reporters—and theirs was the larger faction—it appeared that she would make better copy as the beautiful and tragic form involved in mysterious danger, innocent, but entangled! They loved to print pictures of Beatrice Wilton in her softer humors, to show the exquisite delicacy of her profile, to show her smile, and the large eyes looking down! They combed her past and found it fragrant. Scandal never had touched her. They hunted down her schoolfellows and interviewed them, and learned from them all that was kind and good about their old school companion. They picked up little ancedotes. They printed columns and columns. They stole from one another. They invented, refurbished, decorated, and gilded these tales of Beatrice Wilton. They loaded the telegraph lines with the tidings of her. They photographed her house, her room, her garden—particularly that dark spot where her uncle had been found dead—her horse, her dog, her saddle. Nothing was too minute to deserve attention if it had once belonged to Beatrice Wilton. If she had but looked on a thing. it became of value.

That was not all. They could not very well stop short with Beatrice, but they went on to all the other figures in the case, and made them interesting enough. There was the story of Everett Wilton, of course, rich, happy, young—as men of affairs go—and yet a suicide. Perhaps a suicide because of the blow that had fallen upon his fortune when the *Princess Marie* sank. Could it be that in the mind of Beatrice Wilton there had been some motive of sheer revenge for the same reason? At least, it helped to make one side of the case stronger.

Furthermore, they could take up Doctor Layman, the betrothed of the girl. He was a great help to her. The hostile sheets made little of him, and refused to give him much space, but the friendly journals dwelt at length upon his steadfast devotion. The hours he spent near the jail. His constant visits to the prisoner. His hours of consultation with the lawyer. And, above all, his calm, aloof, aristocratic manner. He was the soul of honor; his straight, steady eyes told what this man was. And could it be dreamed that he would cling to a murderess? Stuff and nonsense! A gentleman of breeding and of position has better taste and better fortune, let us hope! So they spread the doctor at large across their sheets. He made an excellent figure for the photographers. His lean face and pronounced, handsome features always reproduced well, and he was the more desired because he had courteously and firmly requested the reporters to take and print no more pictures of him. Of course, that made the shutters click far more busily than ever.

Then there was the quiet sheriff, he who was known to be the force behind the arrest and the prosecution of the girl. He had collected terrible, deadly facts. He

121

was a man of flawless repute. He could not be accused of partisanship. And yet he stood indubitably against Beatrice Wilton, a vast weight upon the side of her guilt. He no longer even pretended that he was hunting the trial of Fennel—which was mute proof that he believed the girl was the criminal!

Pete Lang, also, came in for his share of notoriety. First of all, he was a rough fellow of the range; and, secondly, he had been the first at the side of the murdered man.

Some newspapers even suggested that, since he had been the first at the dead body—since no one had seen the dead man fall—why might not Peter Lang be the guilty man?

Consider, for instance, that he was a marksman of skill, and that the bullet had been planted squarely, fairly, between the eyes of Wilton. As for motive? Well, motives are rarely known until they are confessed, and being employed by Wilton, it might well be that a testy word had been enough to bring the cowpuncher's revolver out of his pocket! And then he had caught the fancy of the reporters by saying bluntly: "I hope I'm nearer to guilty than she is!"

But not even the fine form of Peter Lang, or the murdered man, or Layman, or the famous sheriff, or the mysterious Fennel, or even Beatrice Wilton herself, so seized upon the imagination of the public press as did another, unaccused figure. And that was Lewis Sherry.

As for photographs, they flooded the papers with pictures of him. They showed him mounting and dismounting. "He makes every horse look small." They showed him walking down the street, towering above Pete Lang. "And yet Lang is nearly six feet tall." They gave the dimensions of his shoulders, the span of his hand, and his weight.

He became in a few days as physically well known as the person of the world's champion pugilist, and his handsome head was nearly always included on the same page with Beatrice Wilton. They made both a harmony and a contrast; lion and panther, as some reporter suggested.

And when they came to delving into the past of this man of the range, the reporters found enough to glut their typewriters and crowd the telegraph wires. He was the hero of many fights; he was the hero of many deaths. And every fight was set down in detail, and every wound was recounted.

He, too, they said, was a hearty advocate of the girl's.

And was he not more than that? And, suppose that she was condemned, would not the giant strike in her behalf, even if it brought about his own ruin?

To big Lew Sherry they could apply all the pet terms of Western literature. He was the "desperado," the "gun-fighter," the "killer," this "brave and reckless man," this "outlaw." And they went on and coined other terms of their own.

Lew Sherry tried not to notice these things, but he could not help it. Clayrock was simply littered with copies of Eastern newspapers containing these accounts; and the home journals also began to boom the issue with all their might. The *Bugle* was on the side of Beatrice Wilton, and therefore, Lew Sherry was a gentle hero. The *Morning Blast* was against the girl, and therefore, to it Lew Sherry was a probable villain.

He called on the editor one day. People fled before him. Doors slammed and crashed. Many footfalls scurried up and down. But when he came to the editor's office he found a little squint-eyed man who wore dark-cloth guards over the sleeves of his shirt, like a grocery clerk, and who peered up to him from beneath a green eye shade.

"What do you want of me, Sherry?" he asked.

"I want you to stop this nonsense," said Sherry.

"Do you?" said the editor. "And can you tell me any reason why I ought to stop it?"

"For the sake of common sense and decency, for one thing," said Sherry.

"Common sense and decency are all very well," said

123

the editor, "but I wish you would point out a time when they were worth balancing against a growing circulation. I've trebled this paper's circulation inside of the last week. I've made it the biggest sheet in the county. And I'm going to keep it there—as long as Lew Sherry will furnish me with good copy, as he's doing today!"

And suddenly a pair of cameras clicked in the corner of the room and Sherry, with wild words, turned and fled more swiftly than from the mouths of cannon.

He went to the sheriff, even, and dourly demanded that these libels should be stopped.

"I'm a peaceful man!" said Sherry. "They're making me out a crook and a general all-around bad actor."

"Steady, steady!" said the sheriff. "After a few more days of this, you'll know what it means to run for office, for instance!"

CHAPTER TWENTY-THREE

LET CRIME increase and follies spread, the press must still be free. And when Sherry had mastered that slogan and understood it might not be altered, he gritted his teeth and made no further protest. But, when a camera man one day pointed a machine too closely at him, he picked up the heavy and expensive offender and heaved it after the artist. Man and machine rolled in the dust, and Sherry stood over them.

"The next time I'll use a quirt on you," said Sherry. "And the time after that—I'll use my hands!"

It almost frightened the camera man to death, but it did not prevent others from clicking pictures of him as busily as ever. It furnished much grist to the papers,

124

moreover. "I'll use my hands!" said a caption beneath an actual photograph of the big paws of Lew Sherry.

A weight of care descended upon Sherry as he saw this tide of publicity in his direction, day after day.

"Trouble is going to come out of it," he assured his friend Lang. "Some young fools are going to come up here to make a reputation out of me. A short cut to headlines is what I offer to anybody who can drop me! And a bullet from behind wouldn't be wasted, either!"

"Sure," agreed Lang. "When you go out, I'll go along with you every time. I'll watch your back for you. But I figure the same as you. The more that's said about a man, the nearer he is to his last picture! But hang the newspapers, say I. Did you see the last lingo that they printed about me? About me having a busted heart of a long-lost sweetheart and a lot of stuff that would've made you creep only to read it, old-timer."

The giant grinned broadly.

"I half believe that you sent 'em up that trail," growled Pete Lang. "Come on with me. We're going to finish the house today."

They had searched it from the top downward. To the room of Oliver Wilton, of course, they devoted their utmost care.

"Of course, he made it like a safe, because he had it lined with stuff that was worth getting!" said Sherry; therefore, they spent two days going over every crevice of the place and tapping every inch of the walls.

But they discovered nothing.

Then they worked down through the other chambers of the house. No one disturbed them. The servants had been discharged, according to Layman's plan, and Layman himself, coming out to the place now and again for books or papers for Beatrice Wilton, was the only one they encountered. He was curious, at first, as to the reason of their stay in the house. But when they evaded his questions rather pointedly, he did not press them. Only he said to Sherry, one day: "Do you think, my friend, that you are doing any good for Beatrice Wilton by tying her name to all your old adventures?"

"Am I dragging her through the dust?" asked Sherry with some sharpness.

"Come, come," said the doctor with perfect good humor. "You understand what I mean, of course. I know that you boys want to do nothing that isn't for her good, but the fact is that you are making a whale of a lot of talk, and the more talk the worse for Beatrice. It's openly said that you're hired by me to be on hand in case we want to beat the law at the last moment. Of course, that is going to be a weight on the minds of the lawyers who will fight for her."

"You want me to hit the trail?" asked Sherry.

"Exactly," said the doctor, who was the most frank of men.

"If I could," said Sherry. "I'd do it. But the fact is that I have to stay. I can't break away. I've tried to before, and it's against my nature."

So the doctor no longer pressed upon that point. To Pete Lang he was rather an offensive personality. But Sherry liked him for the very coldness of mind which troubled Lang. Whatever else the doctor might be, he was a man.

On this day they had no interruption from anyone, even from Layman. They had worked from the top of the house down, leaving the cellar to the last. It had been their major hope from the moment they gave up the room of Wilton as a possibility, and now they attacked it with the greatest care. There was a large wood room under the house, two big storage chambers for the stowage of supplies, and in the front of the house, where the slope of the land allowed windows to be placed, there were two empty rooms—for servants, no doubt—which never had been used. The windows were stuck shut by the strength of the first and last coat of paint which had been applied to them.

Through these chambers, and through the corridors connecting them, they went with methodical attention, searching, rummaging, tapping.

"You don't have to have a barrel to hide half a million dollars' worth of pearls!" Pete Lang was never tired of cautioning his friend.

But when darkness came in the cellar and they had finished the wood room by dint of moving at least a cord of piled firewood, Pete Lang himself confessed that they were wrong. The pearls were not in the house!

It was a great blow to them. As Lang said, the logic all pointed to one conclusion. If the pearls were not in the house, then where were they? Certainly, Wilton had not left his room to secure the supply which was in his pocket when he met Fennel.

"You remember," suggested Sherry, "the talk that Beatrice Wilton said she overheard in the wood between her uncle and a man whose voice sounded like Layman's? Wilton said that he hadn't 'them.' He was excited and angry about it. What did he mean by 'them' unless he meant the pearls?"

"You talk, kid, like a book," admitted the other. "Wilton lost 'em, then? All except a few that he had handy about him, sort of like keepsakes. Is that it?"

"That's the sense of it."

"And what would Layman know about them?"

"He's an old friend of the family."

"How old?"

"Some years at least. He was doctor for both the Wiltons."

"It may not have been Layman's voice at all," said Sherry at last. "If it had been, she wouldn't have merely guessed. She would have known. The things that we *think* we recognize are a long way from the reality. We never have any real doubt about the truth!"

To this Lang agreed, and it was not hard to furnish another character to the man who had conversed with Wilton in the forest behind the house.

It seemed apparent, of course, that Wilton had in his possession—or had had until he lost them—a quantity of pearls or other things of price to which someone besides himself could lay claim. At least, he had not more than a parital interest in the treasure. The strange demeanor of Harry Capper, for instance, could be explained in this manner, as also the odd demands of Fennel, the drunkard and sham.

"If ever we could know the true story of what happened aboard the *Princess Marie*," said Lang, "then we'd be a lot nearer home. But the next thing for us to think about is how we're going to get funds. We can't very well beg them from Beatrice Wilton."

Sherry flushed at the mere thought.

"We have the pearls that were meant for Fennel," he suggested.

"That's State property, by right," objected Lang.

"We can take one of them. How many are there altogether?"

"Five good-sized ones, eleven smaller ones, and eighteen little pearls," said Lang.

"You've counted them pretty well, Pete."

"I've spent some time looking at them, son. They're worth it."

"I'll take one of the bigger ones," said Sherry, "and hock it at one of the pawnshops. D'you know what one of these things is worth?"

They selected a pearl together.

"I dunno," said Lang. "I sort of remember Sam Hulman having a pearl that looked about that size in a scarfpin. Sam, he paid down a hundred and fifty dollars for it. I suppose that you ought to bet about a hundred, for this one."

"A hundred it is," answered Sherry. "It's stealing from something or someone—but not altogether from Wilton. So here goes!"

With that, he went straight down to Clayrock and entered beneath the sign of the Three Moons which showed over the entrance of a shop on the main street. It was littered with the usual assortment of cheap watches and good ones, flashy huge jewelry of paste, and smaller stones of price. Lumbermen and miners had left some of the gilt of their flooding boom days here in the dark shop. There were even jeweled revolvers, pawned at last by some hungry dandy of the frontier!

128

The place was run by a brisk, young man with an open, frank eye, and a fearless cheerful demeanor. He greeted Sherry with a broad smile.

"Evening, Mr. Sherry. Haven't been expecting you, but I never know when the big men of town may pay me a call. Are you buying or selling, Mr. Sherry?"

Sherry looked at him in some hesitation. He was much inclined to find a pawnshop where his name was not so well known, but after a moment of thought he realized that his picture and his name had been spread so thoroughly through Clayrock that it would be impossible for him to remain in the dark.

"I've come to sell," said he, and laid the pearl on the counter.

"And the price?"

"Suppose I leave that to you?"

The pawnbroker took the jewel, passed it under a magnifying glass, and turned it quickly. Then he replaced the pearl gently on the counter.

"Not a bad one," said he. "Suppose I say a hundred dollars?"

The price was exactly what Sherry had been led to expect he might get, and now the closeness of Lang's guess made him exclaim with a broad smile: "Well, I'm dashed!"

But the pawnbroker started.

"Hold on," he said, growing a little red and hurried, "maybe there isn't such a flaw as I thought, and—"

He examined the pearl again. This time he carefully weighed it on a slender scale.

"Matter of fact," he said candidly, "I've made a mistake. I can pay you two fifty, for that."

Sherry scowled.

"I'll take not a cent under five hundred!" said he.

The youth sighed, opened a cash drawer, and laid a bundle of bills before him.

"Well," said he, "I can't drive sharp bargains with you, Mr. Sherry."

CHAPTER TWENTY-FOUR

THE LARGENESS of this price still half stunned Sherry; the value of all the pearls in his pocket suddenly was enhanced; he was carrying about with him what would be a tidy little fortune to many a man. Moreover, the broker did not seem at all displeased with the bargain he had struck, but spread his hands upon the counter and beamed on Sherry as the latter stuffed the bills into his wallet.

"If I'd asked a thousand," said Sherry, "you'd have paid it just as willingly!"

"There's pearls and pearls," answered the other. "Most of 'em that size wouldn't be worth five hundred, even. But this is a beauty. I'll send it East. And maybe the selling price of it even in the trade will scare a thousand dollars to death!"

His frankness made Sherry smile, and the broker smiled back. He was an extraordinary young man, who seemed to make no attempt to cover his pride in his own shrewdness.

"You and Oliver Wilton keep the same sort of pearls in your pockets, I see!" said he.

"Wilton?" exclaimed Sherry.

The pawnbroker narrowed his eyes ever so little.

"Does that surprise you a lot?" he asked.

"Why," said Sherry, "I don't see why Wilton should want to be selling pearls down here!"

"Pawning, not selling. There's a pair of 'em."

He took out a small tray, lined with blue velvet, and upon it were scattered pearls of several sizes. Two big ones lay in the middle.

"That's the couple." He added: "Wilton knew their value, too!"

"Wilton's not apt to redeem the tickets," said Sherry dryly.

And he went out into the blast of the sun's light and heat still blinking and wondering. Why should Wilton have needed money? A good deal of money, at that! For the pair of pearls were both much larger, and fully as fine, it appeared, as the one which he had just sold.

With that in his mind, he hurried back to find Lang, and to him he confided the truth about the price of the pearl. It staggered the man of the range. Together, they laid out the pearls and examined them afresh. If one of them had been sold for five hundred and was worth close to a thousand, the whole of the little collection was now worth a greatly enhanced price.

"If there are many more of these, somewhere," said Lang, "It's a treasure, Tiny. Trouble has popped on account of them. Trouble is going to pop again! But where could Wilton have put the things—or lost 'em?"

They were wandering through the garden of the Wilton house as they talked, for the house was hot, and in the garden a breeze stirred beneath the trees.

"This stuff is worth too much to be carted around in a pocket," said Sherry. "I'll take it back to our room and stow it away. Be somewhere around here, and I'll come back."

Going back to their room, he chose a simple hiding place. A handkerchief made a pouch; he secured the loose edges with a bit of string, thrown over in a pair of half hitches, and he simply dropped the handkerchief into the pocket of an old raincoat which he used on cold, windy days, riding herd. If a search was made for any object of value, it would be a clever man indeed who thought of dipping his hand into the pocket of a dusty old coat. And even if a hand reached into the pocket, the handkerchief might not be examined.

Contented with his own cleverness, Sherry went out into the garden and hurried to find Lang again, he would make that keen fellow guess at the hiding place he had chosen and then enjoy some sort of a small triumph, for Lang was apt to smile with superior wisdom at the simplicity of his big friend. So, in his haste, Sherry cut straight for the point at which he had left Lang, and leaving the path and its crunching gravel, he headed across a stretch of the lawn and came in under the shadow of the trees in time to hear a voice growl:

"Back him up against that tree, Jerry. Watch him. He's got his weather eye peeled on you. That's better!"

Sherry slipped like a great cat among the big trunks of the pines, and so he came on a view of Pete Lang, backed against a large tree, his hands above his head, while one man covered him with a short-nosed revolver, and a second was in the act of reaching for Lang's gun.

"Drop your guns," said Sherry in his deep, booming voice. "And shove up your hands!"

The two started violently. Half sheltered behind a tree, Sherry waited, ready with bullets if they were needed; but neither of the pair attempted to turn upon him.

"He's got the wind of us, Jerry," said Bud.

"He has," said Jerry. "It's the big boy, at that. We gotta strike our sails, Bud, to this squall!"

And, with that, he dropped his gun and raised his powerful arms unwilling above his head.

Bud followed that good example, and Lang, relieved of pressure, instantly covered them with his own pair of weapons. Steadied and helpless beneath the noses of those big Colts, the strangers remained calmly enough while Sherry searched them. He took from each a dangerous-looking sheath knife, and from Bud another short-nosed gun, which was in a hip pocket.

"These are town guns, boys," said Sherry. "You shouldn't carry them out into the big open spaces! Back up there against that bank," he added. "You can put your hands down. if you want to. But mind you, we mean business. If you try to make a break, I'd have

132

as little hesitation in dropping you as in shooting at a pair of tree stumps."

"Aw," said Bud, "we know you! Everybody knows you. I'm gunna make no break!"

He was a little square-made man, with a bright, cheerful face and small eyes that were filled with life. His friend was in exact contrast—a chinless, lean fellow, with a kink in his neck, and an Adam's apple which worked prominently up and down. He allowed Bud to do the talking; indeed, his eyes were constantly seeking the face of his stubbier companion as though to win inspiration.

"We'll get on, then," agreed Sherry. "You two fellows were sent here by who?"

"By no one," said Bud.

"Bud," said Sherry, "are you going to try to pull the wool over our eyes?"

Lang broke in: "There's a mighty right little jail here in Clayrock, and a sheriff that ain't partial to holdup men. You may've heard of Sheriff Bert Moon? Try to come one on us, and you hit the trail for jail and the pen afterward. Come clean, and we turn you off."

"Hold on," protested Sherry. "We have them now. We may wish like anything that we had them later."

"What do they matter?" asked Lang sternly. "They'll never bother either of us again, I have an idea. And we want to get at what sent them here. Bud, who sent you along?"

"We sent ourselves," declared Bud.

"That," said Lang bluntly, "is a lie. I never saw either of you before. You can't have anything against me."

"We got nothing against you," agreed Bud, "but you got something of ours on you."

"And what's that, Bud?"

"What did you leave down in the pawnshop?" asked Bud.

Lang stared at Sherry.

"You're a pair of 'em, are you?" he asked.

133

"From the *Princess Marie?* Sure we are?" said Bud.

"This gets richer and richer," said Sherry. "You're off the *Princess Marie*, then?"

"We are."

"You sailed under Captain Wilton?"

"Yes, he was the skipper."

"And no one sent you here?"

"Nobody. Who would? Lord knows we hunted far enough before we spotted the place where Wilton lived, and we come along too late to find him alive— the sneakin' low hound! That's what he was, a dead beat and a hound!"

That speech was from the heart; there was no doubt about that. And the face of Jerry, as he listened, wrinkled in savage disgust and sympathy.

"You sent yourselves here?" asked Lang, beginning to take charge of the conversation.

"We done just that. It took time. We was clean broke. Working a short job, here and there, picking up what coin we could, we've had a long beat to windward, but just when we'd weathered the point—here comes the big boy with his pair of gats and sticks us up on a reef again. It's tough, I say."

"It's tough," agreed Jerry sadly.

"You came for what's your own?"

"I came for that."

"And what goes to each of you?"

"Five of the big boys, like you pawned; eleven of the middle-sized ones and a bunch of the little fellers," said Bud with instant readiness.

Sherry glanced at Lang, and Lang returned the look with interest.

"What would that come to in cash?"

"About seven thousand iron men," said Bud.

He sighed and rolled up his eyes at the thought of such a fortune.

"How many were aboard the *Princess Marie?*" asked Lang.

"Outside of the chief engineer and Capper—he was

actin' first—and the skipper, there was seventeen of us."

"Seventeen times seven makes about a hundred and twenty thousand dollars."

"Or more, according to how good a market we could find," insisted Bud. "Look here, you and big boy. We got no grudge agin' you. You got the stuff. All right! Let it go at that. All we ask for is our right share. We done our work, didn't we? Look at me! It was me that was the last man aboard the boats! By rights, I'd ought to have something extra. Well, I ain't yelling for that. Only, we want our square cut. Nothin' more! Is that fair?"

'What made you think that we had the pearls?" asked Sherry.

"Would a pair of punchers off of the range be sporting pearls like that?" asked Bud bluntly.

'Sit down, old son," invited Lang. "We want to hear your yarn about the *Princess Marie*."

"Sure," said Bud willingly. "I'll tell you. Not as if you didn't know!"

CHAPTER TWENTY-FIVE

THE ACCOUNT of Bud was straightforward enough, though filled with a good many inconsequential details such as a sailor cannot free his tongue of. He told how he and his companion, Jerry, had shipped on board the *Princess Marie* in San Francisco harbor.

"She was a fine-lookin' hooker," said Bud. "I never ask no better. A good fo'c's'le—roomy enough, and air enough to keep your duds dry in wet weather, buckin' head winds. We never had no kick, to speak of. The skipper was a gent that kept aft and let the men keep forward. We wasn't undermanned. Overmanned, if anythng. The chuck was prime. The watches was regular. Only Capper was a brute. He sailed second, but the first was sick most of the way and he died before the voyage was over. Then Capper, he got the run of the ship, pretty much."

At Hongkong they discharged their cargo and ran down to Singapore looking for another. A week was wasted, sweltering at Singapore, before they went on to Colombo. Here and at Madras, they picked up a cargo and started for Kuching in Sarawak, Borneo, where they discharged part of it and took on some more.

And here it was, apparently, that the captain received his grand idea. Manila was given out as the next port of call, and they bucked up the north Borneo coast into the teeth of a heavy gale. Instead of holding on their course north of Palawan, and straight for Manila harbor, the *Princess Marie* was now turned through the Balabac Strait and went humming south for the Sulu Islands.

That same day, a number of boxes, small but heavy, which had been taken aboard at Kuching, were brought up on the deck and opened. They proved to contain fine new rifles and two machine guns.

Then Capper went forward and exposed the boxes and their contents to the whole assembled crew. He made a speech in which he pointed out that he had been for years about the Sulu Islands; he knew the people and he knew the pearl fisheries, and of one in particular he had heard that it was ripe for investigation. Great stacks of oysters were now in the sheds; the place was manned by not more than three or four whites, and the natives would never stand up to gunfire. For that matter it was doubtful if there were more than half a dozen rifles at that station.

The proposal of Capper was simple and to the point. He suggested that they come up toward the fishery, anchor behind a masking point of land, and under cover of the dark, go in with two of the boats and raid the place. They could capture it at the first rush, shooting into the air. After that, twenty-four hours of brisk work would place in their hands the cream of the spoils of the fishery.

The crew agreed readily. It was Capper himself who had selected the men in San Francisco, and he had taken aboard a choice gang of hardy fellows, who would stop at nothing. They were offered, now, one half of the total haul; the other half was to be split up among the officers, the share of Wilton, as skipper, being a quarter of the whole—not too large a portion, taking into account the fact that he was handling the ship and assuming the responsiblity.

The first mate, still very ill, now gathered strength enough to come on deck, and there before the men he made a hot appeal to them all to pay no more attention to the captain and the second, so far as this raid was concerned, but to remember that these waters were alive with revenue cutters, and that there was very small chance that they could ever get away with their loot in the face of wireless and telegraphs, which would soon give out the alarm.

However, the captain ordered the mate into his cabin, and none of the crew were shaken in their resolve. They looked upon this expedition more or less as the buccaneers looked in the old days upon an incursion into the Spanish main. It was partly piracy, of course, but chiefly it was a grand old lark!

A note of seriousness was struck the very next morning, when it was discovered that the mate was no longer aboard. Capper stirred about among the men and pointed out that the mate had been sick for a long time, that his mind had been upset by the plan to raid the pearl fishery, and that he must have stepped to the rail and dived over during the night.

However, there was a dark feeling among the men that Capper must have taken the affair in hand and tapped the mate upon the head, and then passed him over the rail. There was no suspicion attached to the skipper on this occasion.

However, it was noticeable that Capper, from this day forward, had almost as much control over the ship as the skipper himself. He gave orders. He even argued with Wilton before the men, and the captain put up with it, as though perforce!

In the meantime, they were logging south in the most leisurely fashion, the engines barely turning over enough to give steerage way, and the ship rolling heavily and sluggishly while the crew hastily worked a coat of paint over her. Her color was completely altered, the bands upon the smokestack were changed, and the big letters of the name on the stern were painted out and replaced by *The Dove, of Bristol*.

This name, for a ship which was about to make such a predatory swoop, amused the men highly. At length, the painting was completed, and very late in the afternoon of the next day they ducked inside a coral reef and came to anchor in smooth water to the south of a jutting point of land.

With the darkness, the two boats put off. Only three men were left on board, under the command of the boatswain. The rest, sixteen in number, with the captain in the sheets of the larger boat, rowed in around the point, with muffled oars. In the bow of each boat there was a machine gun. Capper was handling one. Bud himself had the other. In case the station developed unexpected strength, the machine guns were to cover a retreat.

The landing was perfectly simple. That night the sea was almost totally quiet, and with silent oars they pushed on until the prows quenched their speed in the white sand which gleamed faintly under the tropic stars.

They made straight to the station, unchallenged, and then charged in with devilish yells, shooting into the air, as Capper had suggested. Not a hand was raised to oppose them!

By midday of the following day, they had finished their work and were lugging at the oars on the way back to the ship which, having been flagged in the meantime, had worked up steam. And yet they made no great haste away from the island.

As they were turning to come out through the gap between the reefs, a few riflemen came down to the shore and, hiding behind rocks, opened a desultory fire —not as though hoping to delay the ship, but simply in blind anger, to inflict some loss upon her.

However, a few bursts of fire from the machine guns quieted the marksmen ashore, and *The Dove, of Bristol* drew slowly away.

However, they had barely made offing from the island when smoke appeared on the horizon and came up toward them, hand over hand. At full speed, *The Dove, of Bristol* rushed north. The other vessel instantly changed course. There was no doubt that she was pursuing!

Full speed for the *Princess Marie* made little difference. The lookout presently described a long, low hull beneath the smoke cloud of the other ship; it was a government cutter slicing the water like a knife and literally walking over them.

Capper, pale, and stern, and despairing, stood on the bridge and cursed with helpless rage. The captain retired to the chart house; everyone thought that he had funked the issue.

But presently he altered the course due east.

The pursuer was hull up, by this time. It was late afternoon. The sun hung not twice its own breath above the horizon; and then a mutter ran through the crew that they were heading straight for a nest of reefs through which no ship in the world could possibly find a passage.

This murmur grew. The boatswain was made spokesman to go aft and complain to the skipper about the madness of the present course. At which Wilton came out and made a quiet speech. He pointed out that they were totally lost. They could not escape from the government boat by holding straight on their course. Darkness was about to drop over them, but, shortly after, the searchlight of the pursuer would pick them out, and soon a shell would whistle over their heads and thus force them to heave to.

He proposed to head the ship straight on toward the reefs, and as soon as the darkness came, he would open the cocks of the ship, and as she sank, steaming ahead, the boats would be manned. True, the reefs could not be passed by a large ship, but it would be child's play to get through them with the boats.

The crew, astonished by this bold suggestion, cheered their skipper. And all was done as he had conceived the scheme. Darkness dropped. The searchlight of the cutter began to fumble vaguely at the blackness, the *Princess Marie* settled low in the water, and when her decks were almost awash, the boats were shoved off and the oars swept them away. They had not gone a hundred yards, when the *Princess Marie* put her stern in the air and dived from view.

That same night a tremendous storm blew up; they landed to escape the force of a hurricane out of the north. When it had blown over the next morning, they pursued their way and finally made a port, with a sad story of how the hurricane had overwhelmed the *Princess Marie* on a sunken reef, on which she had broken up as the boats were taken off in the falling of the wind.

But now, while they waited for the coming of the ship which would take them back to civilization, the captain, with the brown satchel in which the pearls were stowed by him, suddenly disappeared from the town.

It was suggested that he might have headed for the far side of the island. A searching party failed to bring him in, and so the fruit of the pearl raid was gathered into his own hands.

The lips of the sailors were sealed. They could not very well confess that they had been robbers before they were robbed; but the prize which had been stolen from them was sufficiently large to make every one of them desire to take vengeance into his own hands. Others, no doubt, would follow the trail of Bud, and

Jerry, and Capper, to Clayrock, and trouble was bound to continue until the men had got their dues.

Such was the strange story of the sinking of the *Princess Marie*.

"Wilton's gone," said Bud in conclusion. "He had a brain, but he was a crook. And finally he got his! And now, big boy, we want to know where we come in."

CHAPTER TWENTY-SIX

IT WAS necessary for the two confederates to stare at one another again, as in consultation, after which Sherry said: "This fellow is square, Lang."

"He's square," admitted Pete Lang, "but I don't see what difference that makes."

"I'm going to come clean to him," said Sherry.

He said suddenly to the sailors: "You fellows can hear what I have to say. I don't think you'll believe me, but here goes: When Lang, here, found that Wilton lay dead in the grass, he discovered a handful of pearls in Wilton's pocket. There were five big pearls, and eleven of a middle size, and a number—seventeen, I think—of little ones. He took those pearls and didn't turn them in to the sheriff. For a good many reasons."

"You fool!" barked Lang at his friend. "Do you realize what you're saying?"

"I know what I'm saying," said Sherry. "But what's the use? Are we going to murder these fellows? I think not! And as long as they're alive they'll keep on troubling us—they and the rest of the crew behind them. Let me talk straight out."

"You see what you've got to say?" muttered Lang.

141

"I see, and I'll say it," retorted Sherry.

He continued to the two sailors, who now were as keen as lynxes.

"I'm not going into the thing any more in detail. I'm simply going to ask you to believe that we wern't stealing for ourselves. We were—"

"Hold on," said Lang. "I dunno that I shouldn't have my say about that. Why haven't we as good a right to the stuff as any other man?"

"Hey!" put in Jerry, his voice ringing with indignation. "Did you go to all the trouble of swiping 'em? Did you have a ship sink under you? Did you have a typhoon blow up over your heads? Did you go wanderin' around broke for months, tryin' to locate the snake that had double crossed you? And here you come up sayin' that you got an equal right to them pearls! Is that logic, partners?"

He spread out his lank hands. Jerry was wounded to the heart.

"You swiped 'em," said Lang brutally. "I swipe 'em back. What you gotta say about that? Nobody owns 'em but the fishery. That's the straight of it. Where do you come in? If you steal a hoss does that make you have any claim to the hoss—or to a rope to stretch your neck with? How's that for logic?"

It was such convincing logic that Jerry sat back and bit his lips nervously. His eyes worked this way and that, but troubled though his soul might be, he could not find for it any relief in words.

Both the sailors sat bolt upright and stared at the pair—silenced but deeply hostile.

"Logic's not what we want here," said Sherry. "We want friendliness. And here's where I bid for it."

"If you didn't swipe the stuff," asked Bud angrily, "how come that you sold one of the pearls and hoved the money in your wallet?"

"Because we had to have something to live on while we're working on this case."

"And what call have you got to work on this here case?"

"To prove that Beatrice Wilton is not guilty," said Sherry with much earnestness.

"Say, Bud," said Jerry in some disgust. "Ain't you heard nothin'? Don't you know nothin'?"

With this, he nodded at Sherry in a good deal of friendly sympathy, and the big man flushed darkly. His secret was known, then. Well, for that matter he had seen a thousand hints in the newspapers. He was "the knight of Beatrice Wilton," among other titles showered upon him.

"But we couldn't draw down pay for sitting still, could we?" asked Sherry; "you understand, boys, that we had to live if we were to help. So we soaked one of the pearls. I'll do more. I'll show you the rest of the ones that we have."

"Sure!" said lean-and-lank Jerry.

"It ain't necessary," put in Bud with dignity. "I can tell when a gent is comin' clean with me. I'll take your word big boy!"

"I don't see where all of this rigmarole is heading for!" exclaimed Lang. "It beats me what you got in your head, Tiny!"

"Of course it does," said Sherry with a superior air. "I'll let you in on it now. Do you believe that these fellow were a part of the crew of the *Princess Marie?*"

"Aw, I believe that, well enough."

"Then they'd know the rest of the crew?"

"I suppose so."

"Then they can tell us—and the sheriff—something about Fennel, can't they?"

"Ah, now I foller your drift. But I aim to say that Fennel never was a sailor at all!"

"You're wrong, and you have to be wrong," insisted Sherry. "Fennel was one of the crew; he wanted his split of the pearls; he hated Wilton so badly that when he was close to him, he didn't wait for the split, but murdered him."

"That would be nacheral enough," declared Bud. "But tell me about this Fennel. I've read something about him. Was there any Fennel in the crew, Jerry?"

"There was not, that I knowed of. But we went by front monikers, not the family names. How did he look?"

"Long and thin. A good, big head covered with ratty, ragged-looking hair. Unshaven most of the time. Very fond of his liquor. Clever, too. A sneaking sort of cleverness, I'd say."

The sailors looked gravely at one another, as though reading the books.

"That's Davisson," said Jerry.

"Did he have a scar across his forehead?" asked Bud.

"No. Not a sign of a scar."

"It's not Davisson, then. And if it ain't Davisson, it's nobody from the *Princess Marie*."

"And there you are," said Lang sourly. "You'll be helped on your way a long distance by this, Tiny Lew!"

"Shut up!" answered Sherry angrily. "We've finally established one point: Fennel was *not* a member of the crew. If not, then he was an outside worker. Is that right?"

"And where does that lead you?"

"I don't know. But everything that we learn is something that we know," said Sherry, with a rather childish stubbornness. "What I suggest is this: Get these boys on our side of the fence. If we don't, then when other members of the *Princess Marie* crew hit this town, as they're sure to do, they'll all be waiting for us in a mob, thinking that we have the loot."

"And how'll you get 'em on our side?" asked Lang, still skeptical.

"This way. Boys," he said to the sailors, "I'll offer you a bargain. It may not suit you, but here it is, the best that I can do. You know that the pair of us are doing what we can to help Miss Wilton out of jail, where she doesn't belong. But as sure as there's a heaven, what we do will be no good unless we find this fellow Fennel—or whatever his real name is—and prove that he committed the murder. Otherwise, there's nothing to do except smash open the jail, and you know that jail breaking isn't as easy as opening a can in

144

a town where Sheriff Bert Moon keeps office hours. Are you following me?"

"Like a hound on the trail," said Bud.

"Then throw in with us. This trail goes to sea, where most landsmen can't follow. I think that Fennel's trail goes to sea also. Well, perhaps you could follow it where we can't. Suppose you throw in with us, and Beatrice Wilton is not found guilty—then we turn over to you these pearls. That means six or seven thousand dollars for the two of you. Not your full share, I know. But otherwise, how do you get anything at all?"

Bud said instantly: "Big boy, I'm with you. I like your style fine. I'd sign with you any day. That goes for Jerry, too, Eh?"

"Sure," said Jerry rather vacantly.

"We being broke, though?" queried Bud.

Sherry drew out the wallet, and gave two hundred and fifty dollars into the hand of the sailor.

"That's half the price of the pearl," said he.

Money possesses a peculiar eloquence and emphasis. Now, Bud held the bills in a firm grasp for a moment and stared at them. He had worked most of his life before the mast, and sailors' wages are not high. Then, with a knotted brow, he made exact division and handed half of the whole to Jerry, who was now plainly agape.

"We'll see you through this buster," said Bud quietly. "What do we do first?"

"Go down to Moon and say that you've been sailors. That you knew a man who looked like Fennel. The sheriff will let you see his stuff. Maybe that will tell you something. But right now you can perhaps give us an idea of how many of your other shipmates are apt to turn up here at Clayrock."

Said Jerry: "Three of the boys died in the Sulus before ever they sailed. Budge Sawyer fell from the end of the bridge and busted his back on the way home. Loomis and Cartwright was killed in a dynamite explosion in Frisco right after they landed on shore. Well, that's six out of twenty. The skipper's dead, and so is Capper—and good riddance! And here's me and Bud. Well, say there's ten more that might show up, but will they? I dunno. Some gents are pretty careless. It's a wild goose chase, anyway. I never would've stayed on the road, except that Bud made me. I dunno. I don't think that many more of the crew will be showing up this way!"

Bud said with his grave, bulldog manner:

"Here's my hand, big boy. You, too!"

He shook with Sherry and Pete Lang.

"We're hitting the grit right now. Whatever we find out, we'll let you know. So long!"

And in a moment, they were off down the path.

Lang looked after them with a dubious eye.

"Is there six thousand dollars' worth of brains in that outfit?" he asked. "Is there any chance of getting back what you offer to pay, old son?"

"I don't know," answered Sherry. "But if they're any help at all—great Scott, man, won't it be beyond all price in the world!"

But Pete Lang sighed and looked the other way, like a man dealing with a child.

CHAPTER TWENTY-SEVEN

AFTER THAT, Pete Lang remained at the house; but Sherry, growing nervous with inaction, started into the town to see what he could see, and almost at once encountered the tall form of Doctor Layman, coming along the street with his long, light stride, his trousers brushing together with a *whish* at the knees.

He was white and thin-lipped with anger.

"The sheriff is as full of malice as a mad dog!"

declared the doctor. "By heaven, there's a flaw in the man's mind. He's unbalanced!"

"He's a name for being a square shooter," suggested Sherry, in doubt because of the violence of this accusation.

"Square shooter? He's going to railroad Beatrice to the hangman's rope!" declared Layman. "He's just refused to allow her to see anyone, or even to send out letters! A more high-handed outrage I never heard of!"

"Not even see her lawyers?" asked Sherry.

"And precious lawyers she'll have," stormed Layman, "unless we can get at the funds of the estate. And how is that to be done unless she can execute a power of attorney and place it in my hands—or in any other hands! I've never heard of such illegal tyranny!"

"It is!" said Sherry. He thought a moment and then added: "Some men naturally dislike women. Moon does."

"You're right, of course," acknowledged the doctor. "But there's this to be considered—he never had a chance, before, to put a woman in jail on a heavy charge. And now the tyrant in him is being shown—without precedent."

"Have you appealed to the judge?"

"What use is that? The judge is in Moon's pocket. Everything that Moon does is inspired, one would think. But, by Jupiter, I'm going to break his reputation to bits like bad wood!"

He went on without farewell, only to turn on his heel after a few strides and call back: "You know that Slade—the Phantom, or Fannie, or whatever they call him—is in town looking for you? Is there any bad blood between you two, or is he a friend?

"We've never crossed," added the doctor, and hurried on, like a man full of his own thoughts.

It was a double blow that Sherry had received. In the first place, the news that the sheriff had taken such a pronounced stand against Beatrice Wilton was a shock to him, not only because it was sure to make her way to freedom more difficult, but because it showed

147

from the beginning that Herbert Moon was convinced of her guilt. And the reaction of Sherry was unlike that of Layman. The doctor, keen in the pursuit of the girl's freedom, seemed to have had no feelings except that injustice had been done; but Sherry, looking at the matter in another light, felt the weight of Moon's condemnation. For the sheriff was not a man to make up his mind lightly; and before he would take such a vigorous attitude as that which he had adopted toward the girl, it was certain that he had searched the case thoroughly from beginning to end.

In a word, if Herbert Moon felt that Beatrice Wilton was guilty, guilty she undoubtedly was!

The chief work for Sherry, he resolved, as he marched on down the street, was not to prove her innocent, but to devise means of getting her out of jail. And bitterly, now, he regretted the threats which he had poured upon the quiet little sheriff in the Wilton house, on the day of the coroner's examination. He had, in gambling parlance, tipped his hand, and the sheriff would be waiting for exactly such an attempt as Sherry now had in mind.

However, for the moment even the girl was thrust to the back of his mind. There was another point of great importance, for the nonce. Slade!

His name showed the manner in which he had graduated in the school of violence. Fannie Slade they called him now. But in the earlier days, before debauchery and a thousand crimes had lined his face and put iron in his heart, he had been known as Phantom Slade. Because like a ghost he stepped without sound. And his wild rides across country made his presence ubiquitous.

It was not likely that Slade had come to Clayrock for any friendly purpose. If he were asking for Sherry, it meant that he was intent on making trouble—his vocation in life.

It might well be that the fame of Sherry, so foolishly spread abroad by the pages of many newspapers—his fame as a gunfighter—had come to the ears of Slade and wakened the jealously of the famous killer.

For such was Slade. It was said of him, as of some cutthroats of earlier days, that he killed men merely for the pleasure of seeing them fall. There was no chivalry in Fannie Slade. He would shoot from behind as readily as he would shoot from the front. He had a tiger's indifference to honorable methods of warfare. The tales that were told of him chilled the blood. Though still in the prime of life, he was old as a slayer. He had begun in his teens, said rumor. He was now over thirty. And he was said to have killed a man a year.

It was no wonder that Sherry grew cautious and his manner altered as he went down the street.

All things had now a different meaning. There was as great a contrast as there is between day and night in the mind of a child—or in the minds of most grown men. All had been open and harmless the instant before, but now every alley-mouth yawned at Sherry like a leveled gun, and every open window was a source of careful thought.

For so Slade acted.

Like the rattler, he delivered his warning the instant he appeared. And, by so doing, he more or less established that he was to be the hunted as well as the hunter. The warned man would be sure to be upon his guard, might well be expected to deliver a counter-attack. But Slade trusted to the superior secrecy and cunning of his own maneuvers to gain the upper hand.

However, it might all be another matter. Some mutual friend might have recommended Sherry to Slade. In hope of that, the big man went on. For he had no desire to risk his life in such an unequal battle. It was true that he had a gift of speed and surety with weapons, but he never had given to fighting for its own sake, the professional attention which Slade had devoted to the game. He had lived by labor; Slade had lived by his Colt.

Sherry went straight to the hotel and sat down on

the veranda. It was an empty veranda when he arrived, but quickly it was filled. People turned in from the street in passing; others came out from the building. For everyone was anxious to be in the presence of this temporarily notorious character.

And then his next neighbor leaned a little toward him: "You're in for Slade, I guess?"

"Have you seen Slade?" asked Sherry.

"He's over in Ratner's Saloon."

"Did you see him there?"

"Yep. He lined up everybody and bought a drink."

"He wants me?"

"That's what he says."

"To talk or shoot?" asked Sherry.

"I dunno. What does he usually want when he sends for a gent?"

Sherry was silent; the answer was too obvious.

"The best way is for you to sit tight," volunteered Sherry's neighbor. "You stay put where you are, with plenty of the boys around you. That way, Slade won't have a chance to get behind you."

"Will you do me a favor?"

"Proud an' happy to!"

"Go over to Ratner's Saloon and ask Slade what he wants of me."

The other stiffened a little and changed color. But he was a man of courage.

"I'll do it," said he. "Are you—are you gunna make a show-down of it, Sherry?"

"I'll hear his answer, first," said Sherry.

The other rose, and walked rapidly down the veranda steps. Once in the street, he paused, tightened his belt, jerked his hat on more firmly, and with all the air of a man going to undertake a really desperate commission, he started for Ratner's Saloon, the front door of which was visible across the street some distance down.

Through the swinging door went the messenger, and was gone a mortal minute. Then he appeared again, not walking, but literally hurled through the air. He landed in the street, rolled over and over in the dust,

150

then picked himself up and come on the run back to the hotel.

When he arrived, a crowd gathered around him, but he fought his way through them to Sherry and stood before the latter, a battered, tattered specimen. One sleeve of his coat was missing and a great rent went up its back. His hat was gone. One eye was very red, and rapidly beginning to swell and turn purple.

"I done your dirty work for you, Sherry," he declared angrily. "And a fine reception they gave me! Slade has every ruffian in town around him. When I asked him your question, he said to me: 'Tell the low skunk that I'm here to get him, and that I'm comin' soon! Tell him to be ready! But what are you doin' down here, you sneakin' spy?'

"The rest of them took that up. They dived on me, half a dozen of 'em, beat me up, and turned me out! And you, Sherry, you—what're you gunna do about it?"

He was a young fellow with plenty of fighting spirit, and now, with his fists clenched, he looked as though he were about to throw himself at Sherry's throat.

"Steady, steady!" said Sherry. "Let me have a minute to think this thing over!"

And think it over he did, and in dead silence. Caution told him to wait where he was or, better still, go home to the assured protection of Pete Lang, rather than trust to the motley crew here, where each man was only for himself. Then he looked at the half-obscured eye and the tattered coat of his emissary, and honest anger cleansed the heart of Lew Sherry.

Wait for Slade here? Even policy forbade that he wait in silence, his nerves wearing him thin, while Slade took his ease, and came to strike when he was ready.

He rose suddenly to his feet.

"What you gunna do?" demanded the messenger again.

"I'm going to get you another coat," said Sherry, and went down the steps in one stride.

CHAPTER TWENTY-EIGHT

IT WAS not far down the street to Ratner's place, but it seemed a great distance to Sherry, for he had clothed himself in his wrath as in a garment, and every step that he took increased his anger.

For, after all, it was little short of murder that the great Fannie Slade now contemplated. He must know his own superiority over such a common puncher from the range as Sherry was, but, eager to swell his own reputation by destroying that of this newly rising light, he had come to consume Sherry like a tiger on the trail.

And it maddened the big man to think of the gunman leaning at Ratner's bar, surrounded by his cronies, waiting for nerve to weaken in Sherry. And besides, what strange thoughts, what odd devices, were now rising in the imagination of the destroyer?

A brisk young man jogged a horse up the street and hailed Sherry.

"I've come over from the sheriff's office," said he. "Sheriff Moon knows that Slade is in town. He's heard that Slade is threatening you."

"And what is that to him?" asked Sherry, vexed.

"He sent me to tell you not to go near Slade. It's his business, as sheriff, to handle that man, and he wants no other person to interfere."

Sherry, truly amazed, looked in wonder at the boy. The latter continued:

"Sheriff Moon is waiting for Slade to come out of the Ratner Saloon. He's surrounded by his cronies and his hangers-on, in there, and any of them would as soon shoot a man in the back as look at him in the face. But when Slade comes out, the sheriff will tend to him. He expressly wanted me to tell you this."

"Young fellow," said Sherry, "this is darned kind of the sheriff. Tell him so from me. Who are you?"

"Sheriff Moon is my uncle. I am his sister's son," said the boy. "My name is Charles Crandall."

He was as clean a lad, with as straight an eye, as ever Sherry had seen.

"I didn't expect this from the sheriff," answered Sherry. "I've been rather tough on him. Now I thank him from the heart, but it's too late. I've got to go and get Slade."

He strode on down the street.

But presently he was aware of a shadow following him. He jerked suddenly about and saw that the youth had dismounted and was coming from behind, quietly, and straight behind.

"And now what do you want?" asked Sherry.

"My uncle told me to prevent you from meeting Slade," said the boy.

"Will you prevent me by walking at my heels?" asked Sherry, half annoyed and half wondering.

"No, sir," answered Charles Crandall. "But at least I can help you when it comes to the pinch."

Sherry actually gasped.

"Do you mean that?"

"Yes, Mr. Sherry, of course."

"That you'd go into Ratner's place with me?"

"I'm under orders," said the boy.

"Look here!" exclaimed Sherry. "What are you doing in this town?"

"It's the school vacation," said Charles Crandall. "I came out to visit my uncle, you see."

"And now you're going to take a chance of breaking your neck for yourself? Crandall, I like you fine. You have as much nerve as any youngster I ever heard of, but now I order you to get away from behind me."

He stepped on, looking back over his shoulder; young Charles Crandall remained rooted where he was.

And so Sherry went on again, turning many thoughts in his confused brain, and always harking back to the strangeness of this day, which had brought him a kindly word and a kindly hand from Herbert Moon!

Bitterly, bitterly, he realized what all other men knew, that Herbert Moon was the soul of honor, of courtesy, of human gentleness, and therefore, the case of Beatrice Wilton seemed darker and darker.

And this sorrow, this inner gloom, went to color his anger and make it more savage, until he was cold with rage as he reached the door of the Ratner Saloon.

He paused for an instant and looked up the street, and down it. At either end the people were flooding from their houses and blocking the road with a solid mass of humanity, and still they poured out, like water from every crevice after the long wave has receded to the sea.

He would have spectators for his death, at the least!

Then he struck the door with his fist and dashed it open, and as he did so he was conscious of a shadow just at his back. He glanced like lightning over his shoulder, and saw the handsome face of young Charles Crandall!

It was too late to turn back the gallant boy again! So Sherry stepped on into the saloon, and the first face that his eye fell upon was that of Fannie Slade. He saw that man with a wonderful distinctness in a hundredth part of a second. And it was an unforgettable face, with bright silver tufts of hair at either temple; sunken eyes that flashed like metal out of the deep shadows beneath the brow; and lines of irony and pain and savagery marked on it deeply everywhere.

That face convulsed with anger at the sight of Sherry; but the eyes widened and grew blank, also. Plainly, Fannie Slade was receiving the greatest surprise of his life, and he was not enjoying the shock.

But it is that way many a time; a reputation grows too great. The pedestal becomes so high that even the statue is afraid of falling. So Slade stared, unable to believe that any man dared to invade his lair.

"Are you ready, Slade?" called Sherry.

The great Fannie Slade leaned a little forward, his left hand extended along the edge of the bar, his right hand at his thigh, just hovering over the handles of his revolver, but he did not draw, and he did not speak.

"Keep back, all of you," said a quiet young voice behind Sherry. "I'll start shooting the first man who tries to interfere!"

That was the sheriff's nephew. A bit of real stuff, thought Sherry.

The blankness was leaving the eyes of Slade, but still a ghost of it remained, and suddenly Sherry stepped forward. He dared not stand quietly, waiting for the gunman to make the first move.

"You sent for me, Slade, to tell me that you were coming," said Sherry. "I couldn't keep such a famous man waiting. Here I am."

He stood close, looking down on the slayer.

And then the glance of Slade wavered in a flash to the side—and back again to Sherry. But it told Sherry enough. It was a blinding ray of light.

"Great guns!" said Sherry. "I thought you were a man. I didn't expect to find merely a murdering sneak."

And with his left hand, lightly, he struck Slade upon the cheek. The gun fighter turned white as death; but that deadly and famous right hand remained frozen upon the handles of his gun!

Sherry turned his back and saw a line of sick faces along the bar.

"This is a rotten show, boys," said he. "You'd better get your friend out of town, because I hear that the sheriff may want him!"

And he walked out of the saloon, leaving deathly silence behind him. At his back stepped young Charles Crandall, his revolver still leveled, guarding the retreat of the big man. When they were outside, he sprang before Sherry and wrung his hand enthusiastically.

"That was a grand thing!" cried Charles Crandall. "That was the finest thing that I ever saw or heard of.

Even Uncle Herbert never did a better thing in all his life!"

"You go back to your uncle," said Sherry, "and give him a message from me, word for word. Will you do that?"

"Yes, sir," said Crandall, with an almost soldierly readiness.

"Tell him that he ought to keep you at home, because if you wander around, one of these days you'll blow up."

"I don't know what you mean by that," protested the youngster.

"I don't suppose you do," nodded Sherry. "But *he* will. In the meantime, I want you to know that I'm your friend. I never would have come out of Ratner's alive without you at my back. You don't have to repeat that to the sheriff. I'll call on him and tell him that myself!"

He left Charles Crandall with a face suffused with joy, and went slowly back up the street to the hotel. He did not arrive there first. Hurrying figures had left the saloon shortly after his departure, and they had given brief messages to the curious. So a murmur arose before Sherry and behind him as he went up to the youth of the tattered coat and black eye.

"Young fellow," said Sherry, "I thought that I could get a coat out of the crowd in Ratner's for you. But they didn't want to play. Come into the store with me, and I'll get you a new one!"

A broad grin played over the battered face of the other.

"Partner," he said with emotion, "I wouldn't change this here coat, now, for a broadcloth one—not with tails to it!"

He added, in a burst of enthusiasm: "It don't seem possible that you made Slade take water! Great guns! Fannie Slade! The killer! Now, every terrier in town will take after his scalp!"

"They'll never catch up with him," suggested Sherry. "Slade has sloped, by this time, I think!"

156

And, in fact, Slade had disappeared from Clayrock on a fast horse, and none of his escort of cronies rode with him. But as Sherry went down the street again, he saw that his own position in the town had altered considerably. Men and women had looked at him before with awe, to be sure, but also with dread, as one would admire a huge, but savage dog. But now they regarded him with a more friendly air. Children suddenly darted out of gates and began to tag along behind him. A bold spirit ran past him and slapped at his great ponderous, swinging hand. Sherry scooped him up as he fled and whirled him in the air, while the boy shrieked with fear—and found himself suddenly deposited upon a vast shoulder, then settled safely upon the ground again. So laughter arose and spilled back and forth riotously among the children, and they swarmed around the knees of the big man all the way to the sheriff's house.

It was the smallest dwelling in Clayrock; it was also the most poverty-stricken; but in front of it there was a garden of flowers which the sheriff kept going by much labor in the intervals between his man-hunting expeditions. He was digging in that garden, now, on his knees, whistling cheerfully as he worked around the roots of an ancient rosebush.

"Hey!" shrilled a child in the crowd. "Look what we've brought home to you for lunch, Sheriff Moon!"

And they yelled with delight as Sherry strode triumphantly through the gate.

Sheriff Herbert Moon got up from his knees rather painfully, and with a slowness which made Sherry realize that time was stiffening the hero.

"Well, well, well," said Moon. "I'm glad to see you here. I was sorry to hear from Charles that you had taken such a foolish chance. But, of course, I'm glad that it turned out that way. I never would have dared to go into Ratner's for him, I'm sure! Come into the house and sit down, Sherry!"

So spoke the sheriff, knowing that twenty youthful

ears heard this tribute to Sherry at the speaker's own expense.

And then he led the giant into the little house, where Sherry had to bow his head to pass through the door, and where he hardly dared to stand erect even inside, because the rafters sloped down so low at the sides. Charles Crandall sprang up at the other end of the room.

"You run along," said the sheriff. "You're a little young to hear what we're going to say!"

CHAPTER TWENTY-NINE

THE PLACE looked like a Mexican hut, on the inside. That is to say, the floor was simply hard-packed earth, cool and comfortable in summer, soundless underfoot —but necessarily damp in the winter. There was only one room, but each of the four corners was used as a separate chamber. The stove, with pans and pots hanging behind it, filled one nook; a table, flanked by shelves of dishes and cups and saucers, took the next; the third contained a large roll-topped desk which looked absurdly out of place, but which, as everyone knew, probably contained more valuable information about criminals and criminal life than any depository in the Southwest.

The fourth corner was the sheriff's library, two or three hundred old, time-faded volumes being ranged along the shelves there. Near the desk was one couch, and in the "library" was a second, which supplied the sleeping accommodations. The rear door had been left open by Charles Crandall and, therefore, Sherry was able to look out on the regular rows of a vegetable garden, behind which stood the barn. This was such a pretentious and solid structure that neighbors sometimes asked why the sheriff did not move his horses into his house, while he took up his residence in the stables. But he was apt to say in his good-natured way that his horses were worth much more than his skin.

It was not really a very uncomfortable dwelling, when one's ideas were finally accommodated to this scheme of things. In Mexican style, the floor and the couches and even the chairs were covered with goatskins; on the wall was ranged an armory of weapons, new and old: shotguns of several makes and sizes, rifles, and a whole rack of revolvers, with boxes of ammunition beneath. Regularly, winter and summer, in heat or in cold, the patient sheriff stood in his rear yard and worked two hours with his guns. Neighbors peered over the fence and took note of these exhibitions, and what they saw prevented the world from considering that the sheriff had grown old!

"Will you tell me," said Sherry, "how you can go away on trips and leave all these things behind you? I don't think either of those doors would hold, even if they had locks and bolts and bars, which I don't see!"

"This house is never locked," answered the sheriff.

"Then you've weeded all the thieves out of Clayrock?" said Sherry.

"One lifetime isn't long enough to do that," smiled Herbert Moon. "All that I'm able to do is to cut off the heads of the tallest weeds—keep them from choking out the wheat so to speak. And I suppose that a good many fellows would like to have a look inside my desk, yonder, or put their hands, on those guns."

"You hire someone to guard the place when you're away, then?"

"I can't afford that," said the sheriff. "Besides, who could I trust? But I have better guards than men ever could be. I'll show them to you."

He whistled softly, and instantly two sleek white forms leaped into the doorway and came to their master —two powerfully made bull terriers with snaky heads,

159

and little, dangerous eyes. They stood at attention like soldiers, their cropped ears pricking.

"This is the answer," said the sheriff. "When I'm away, the rear door is wedged open just enough for them to go in and out. They can't be poisoned, for they've been taught to take food from no hand except mine and that of my neighbor, Mrs. Miller. She looks after them while I'm gone, but even Mrs. Miller doesn't dare step into the yard. Once or twice there have been awkward situations when tramps came to beg at the door, but a tramp with a fast bull terrier at his heels can do wonderful jumping. Up to this time, they've always been able to clear the front fence in their stride; but I confess that I'm always relieved when I get home and find that Jack and Jill have hurt no one."

Sherry smiled. He could understand a great deal about this little man by the explanation he had given. For what could have been more effective than such an arrangement? And certainly even those accustomed to danger from men and guns would hesitate to face the teeth of these small white defenders! A wave of the sheriff's hand sent them slipping out of the house again.

Sherry said bluntly: "Sheriff, I've come to talk plain talk."

"I like that kind best," said Moon.

"You've had the name of a square shooter, always. But now you have a girl in jail and you're bearing down on her."

"In what way, Sherry?"

"You've refused to let her see anyone; you've refused to let her send so much as a note out of her cell!"

Herbert Moon did not attempt to deny the accusation, but he said with a nod: "One has to take a different line with nearly every prisoner."

"But what does the law say about this?"

"The law doesn't give me any such power," said Moon with amazing openness. "However, I often have to overstep the bounds of the law."

"Do you admit that?" gasped Sherry.

"In our country," replied the other, "the law is made

160

entirely for the sake of the accused, to assure him of receiving justice. We're raised to believe that all men are free and equal, and according to the letter of the law an accused man, no matter what proofs are against him, is apt to be treated as though he were a little more free and equal than any other person in the land!"

Sherry nodded.

"I follow that," he said. "I don't want to make trouble about this. I'd rather stand behind you, Moon. But—tell me this, sheriff. Are you sure that Beatrice Wilton killed her uncle?"

The sheriff made a little pause at this for, frank as his talk had been, this was a question that rather overstepped the bounds.

At length he answered: "You want a free answer to that—an answer never to be repeated, of course?"

"Of course not," agreed Sherry.

"Then I'm glad to tell you that my mind is entirely made up. It doesn't often happen that an officer of the law can throw himself into his work with surety. But I feel an absolute surety now!"

Sherry sighed.

"I hate to hear this," he admitted. "Is she as surely guilty as all this? Is there no way of throwing a little blame on Fennel?"

"My case is not entirely made up," answered the sheriff. "I'm frank to say that. But the truth is that this crime never in the world would have been committed if it had not been for Beatrice Wilton!"

Sherry loosened his collar and took a great breath.

"I think you're wrong," he said huskily. "But suppose that you get together enough evidence to convince a jury—what will they do with her?"

"Find her guilty of murder in the first degree; but since she's pretty, they'll recommend a mild sentence, or some degree of mercy, I have no doubt."

"And then?"

"I know the judge, I think," replied the sheriff coldly.

"And you'll influence him to give her all that the law allows?"

"A good judge never can be influenced," answered Herbert Moon.

"Man, man!" muttered Sherry. "She's young— A more beautiful woman was never made!"

At this, Moon stood up from his chair.

"A woman born with a pretty face is born with a curse!" said he. "Her beauty becomes her end of living, her vocation. Her work is to let herself be seen. She doesn't need to be witty, or gentle, or kind. She's a tyrant! The world comes to her and bows down. If I were a married man, I'd pray that my daughters should be plain women. As for the beauties—heaven help them!"

"And that's why you hate Beatrice Wilton?" asked Sherry gloomily.

Moon went to him and laid a hand on his shoulder.

"My boy," said he, "I know that your heart is aching over this. I want to do something for you. If it will give you as much pleasure as pain, you are free to go to the jail and see the girl—and talk to her alone."

"Would you let me do that?"

"On one condition, that you take no written message for her from the jail. As many oral messages as you please. But not a syllable in writing."

"It's a good deal to offer me," admitted Sherry. "When may I go?"

"Now, if you wish. I'll send over word to the jailer. And you may see her again, as often as you wish, only promising that you'll never take a bit of writing from her."

"I'll give that promise."

"I'll take your hand on it, Sherry."

They shook hands, and Sherry, his mission performed, left the house in haste.

CHAPTER THIRTY

ON THE way to the jail, Sherry encountered Bud and Jerry, the two sailors ambling cheerfully along through the town. They hailed him with good-humored salutes, and he paused for talk.

"We seen the stuff of this here Fennel," said Jerry. "He was no sailor. He was a farmer! What sailor would have such a bunch of cheap junk? Besides, everything was new!"

"You spotted that for sure?" said Sherry.

"Of course, we spotted it for sure! There's no doubt at all. And all that stuff come out of old Cap Wendell's in San Pedro. He carries that kind of junk. I tried to outfit there once myself!" declared Bud Arthur.

It shocked Lew Sherry with surprise and with delight.

"You could swear to that?"

"I seen one of Cap's labels sticking on an undershirt. Cotton and wool. Nineteen threads of cotton and one of wool. That's the kind of stuff that Cap uses!"

"Boys," said Sherry, "will one of you go out to San Pedro for us?"

"We ship always together," said Jerry.

"Then go out together and talk to Cap Wendell. He might remember something about Fennel."

"And what good would that do? It's a long cruise out there and back," protested Bud.

"Of course it is," agreed Sherry. "But we've lost Fennel's trail here at Clayrock. Wherever he's gone, he's disappeared completely from under our eyes. But this Wendell might be able to tell you what ship

Fennel landed from, and where he intended to ship again. And unless we can get him—a woman is going to hang for a murder that Fennel must have committed. Do you understand that, boys?"

They understood.

"We'll go," said Bud, the controlling spirit of the two. "If we ever can get to windward of Fennel, he'll never weather us, and we can promise you that! When does this here trial begin?"

"Tomorrow."

"A day out and a couple days back. We'll get the news if we can, but Cap Wendell ain't likely to remember any too much. He's a moldy old scoundrel, is Wendell!"

They said good-by on the spot, and Sherry went on to the jail, where the sheriff's message already had been received. The jailer was a grim-looking fellow with a shock of red hair, very tousled, and a hard, white face.

"You play on the inside with Moon, do you?" he asked Sherry. "Well, his orders go here. Come on into the office. I'll bring her in."

"Alone? Can I see her alone?" asked Sherry.

The jailer shook his head.

"It ain't legal," he declared, "but Moon makes up his own laws around these here parts!"

He was gone, and Sherry stood by the window, ill at ease, shifting from one foot to the other, feeling very much like a small boy late for school.

He heard no steps disappear or approach—ample testimony to the soundness of the walls of the building —but suddenly the door opened, and Beatrice Wilton stood before him. The jailer loomed for an instant behind her, grinning strangely at Sherry; then the door closed, and they were alone.

She came hastily across to Sherry, with great relief in her face.

"Eustace sent you!" she exclaimed. "Isn't that it? Eustace finally persuaded the sheriff?"

"No," said Sherry. "I went to Moon and talked to

164

him. He said that I could come and talk to you here."

"You—and not Eustace Layman?" she murmured, greatly amazed. "I don't understand that. But it doesn't matter! It doesn't matter! As long as I can send out a written message by you—you could be a witness to my signature, too! I—Here's a pen and paper!"

She hurried to the desk, almost running, and sat down at it. Then Sherry leaned over her.

"I promised Moon that I wouldn't take out a message—a written message. Anything that you want to send by word of mouth. But nothing written."

She pushed the paper away from her and dropped the pen. She looked up at him quite wildly. Not since she had tried to take her own life when he and the sheriff were in the room had he seen her so completely unnerved.

"You promised him?" she exclaimed.

"I had to, for otherwise he wouldn't have let me come here at all."

She clutched her hands together and her eyes flashed from side to side.

"What can I do then," she muttered. Then, more confidently: "But you won't pay any attention to your promise? Of course you won't! He hasn't a right to treat me as he does! It will take me two minutes to write out the order to the bank. You will take it?"

"You don't understand," said Sherry patiently. "I gave him my word. I shook hands with him on it!"

"What is a promise to a scoundrel?" asked the girl earnestly. "He keeps me here without a chance to talk to a lawyer—except at a distance, watched every minute. I haven't been able to raise a retaining fee. I'm helpless and hopeless. What am I to do? I never can win against Herbert Moon in this town and court without the finest lawyer in the country. And how can I bring in a great lawyer unless I have money? And my money in the bank I can't touch—I can't touch it, because of the sheriff! So you see what he's doing?"

Anguish was depicted on the face of Sherry.

But the voice of Herbert Moon was still, so to speak,

sounding in his ear. He said: "It sounds pretty bad. But I think it will turn out better than you imagine. There never was a squarer man in the world than Moon!"

"Ah," cried the girl, "you think that because you know how he's treated men. You don't know how he'd treat a woman. He's never had a woman before on a serious charge. And now he shows himself for the first time. No, no, not the first time. You can see it through his whole life. He hates women! He hates them!"

"I don't follow you there," confessed Sherry.

"Has he ever wasted his time on any woman or girl in his life? He's never married. Women don't exist for him—except to loathe them!"

"That's happened before," said Sherry, "to men who were married to their guns and their work. Besides, he has such a beggarly poor salary, how could he ask a woman to share his life? Have you seen the house he lives in? A Mexican laborer lives in better style!"

She stared at him with blank eyes.

"You mean that you won't do it, then? You won't carry out a note for me?"

"I can't," said Sherry.

"But," she went on in a bare whisper, "you understand what it means? My life! My life!"

"I understand what you think," said Sherry huskily. "Heaven knows that I want to help you. But I've given him my hand on it—and my promise!"

She drew herself up from the chair and seemed about to break into excited speech; but she suddenly collapsed and dropped her face on her arms, weeping heavily. Sherry drew back from her as though a gun were pointed at him. He looked at the door; he glanced behind him at the window; never in his life had his heart been so wrung.

He could only stammer: "I put my trust in Moon. You'll find that he'll give you a fair chance in the end. It's only now that we don't understand—"

That seemed to sting her back to some self-control and she threw up her head.

"They begin tomorrow. They begin to hang me tomorrow. Oh, mark what I say! The sheriff has the judge in his hand. The weight of the sheriff has poisoned the mind of every man in the county, already! They couldn't pick a jury that wouldn't be ready to hang me. And tomorrow the trial begins! Who have I to defend me? No one but a foolish young lawyer. A man with no experience! And he's doing it on the chance of collecting his fees! I haven't been able to give him any promise in writing. I—I— They've tied my feet and hands and thrown me into a river to swim if I can! Don't you see it?"

He could only stare at her miserably, until at last her own expression of desperation altered to one of horror.

"You think with the sheriff!" she breathed at last. "You think with Sheriff Moon—that I'm guilty!"

He tried to answer, to disclaim, but truth tied his tongue, and forced him to be silent.

"You'd better go," she said, in a trembling voice. "I don't think there's any good in your staying here longer. You'd better go—at once!"

Sherry stumbled toward the door, but with his hand on the cold metal of the knob he managed to turn about and face her again. His brain was reeling.

"I came to ask how I could help," said he. "I shouldn't have come at all. But I want to tell you from my heart that the worst is never going to happen to you. They have thick walls here, but I don't think that they could keep me out!"

"Is that what you came to say to me?" she asked. "That after I'm found guilty and judged to be worthy of hanging—then you'd come to break into the jail and take me away?"

He was silent, and saw her shaking her head.

"I never would go," she said. "Heaven knows that I've no desire to cheat the law!"

Sherry jerked the door open without even a word of farewell and blundered out upon the street. It was blazing hot. The heat waves shimmered upward from the white, uneven dust, and from the whitewashed wall the sun reflected as from a mirror, but it seemed to Sherry the coolest place in the world!

He mopped his brow and went on with the same uncertain step. He found that his lips were twitching; and his eyes, staring before him, continued to see a picture which he knew never would leave him—of Beatrice in the jail, looking on him with a despairing calmness, and denying that last, faint hope of escape.

CHAPTER THIRTY-ONE

HE WAS glad of the distance and the steep slope back to the Wilton house, for it gave him a chance of purging his mind, as it were, by the sheer exercise of physical effort, and he came to the house with a clear brain, at the least, to find, in their small cabinlike room, Pete Lang bent low over a piece of paper.

He looked up at his friend with a sidewise scowl of thought.

"What is it, Pete?" asked the big man, with assumed lightness. "Key to a treasure?"

Lang looked back to his work and made no reply, while Sherry went on: "I've seen the sheriff."

At this Pete raised his head.

"He's straight, to my way of thinking. I never sat and talked to a finer man, Pete."

Lang yawned.

"He even gave me leave to go to the jail and talk to Beatrice Wilton!"

At this, the cowpuncher started.

"Gave you permission?"

"He did!"

"It ain't possible. He wouldn't let Layman go near her."

"It's queer," said Sherry. "I know that it's queer. But up to the jail I went and had a talk to her."

"You say it like you'd been to a funeral."

"I'd promised the sheriff that I wouldn't take any message in writing from her to anyone. Of course, that was the one thing she really wanted me to do."

"It upset her?"

"Of course. They've badgered her and tyrannized over her. I've never heard of any prisoner about to be tried for his life that has had such a rough deal as that girl!"

Lang yawned again.

"Leave me alone," he pleaded. "I'm busy."

"Finally," went on Sherry, "I told her that I'd never leave her to the law, if the decision went against her. What do you think she answered?"

"I don't know; I don't care," said Lang.

"That she wouldn't go a step with any man. That she didn't want anything from the law. Justice, I suppose she meant."

Here Lang favored his companion with a long and earnest stare.

"Is that straight?" he asked.

"That's exactly what she said to me."

"I'm going out for a walk with you," said Lang. "Come along with me, will you?"

"I'm going to sleep. I need a nap. I'm tired."

"You're fresh as a baby compared with how tired I am. Shut up, and come along!"

Sherry, grumbling, obeyed, and they went out to the garden. There in the tool shed, Lang took a strong shovel and handed Sherry a pick.

"Are you going to bury somone?" asked Sherry.

"Shut up," replied Lang. "Foller me!"

He led the way straight back from the house into the woods behind it, and there he headed into the broken ground through which they had toiled with such difficulty on their first day at the Wilton house.

Now, however, Lang moved in a weaving course which kept him going with comparative smoothness and speed.

"How much time have you spent out here solving the labyrinth?" asked Sherry.

But Lang did not answer. He kept to his work, setting a stiff pace, like a man whose brain is in a state of great anxiety. At length he came to a clearing. Into the middle of this he marched and faced toward the north, picking out a tree on that side. From the tree he paced several steps to the south, then turned sharply at right angles and marched in a new direction. He began over again at the southern side of the clearing and wherever his new course cut the old one, he marked the spots with a dig of his heel.

Then, pausing, he considered the last three marks which he had made, stepped away from them, and drove his shovel into the ground with force.

"Try your pick here!" he commanded, and Sherry, now thoroughly in the spirit of the adventure, obeyed at once, burying the pick to the handle.

They began to tear up the ground, working very hard and fast for a half hour. In the course of that time, with pick and shovel, they had opened a deep hole, when Lang leaped out of the excavation and signed to Sherry to refill the hole.

Gloomily, irritated, Sherry obeyed, and after they had piled the dirt in and trampled it down as well as they could, Lang scattered pine needles carefully over the spot and tried to remove all signs that they had been digging there.

"I've missed—for today," said he.

"Suppose you tell me what crazy thing you're up to?"

"Well, this."

He thrust a paper before Sherry. Upon it appeared a rudely sketched outline which might have served for the plan of the clearing in which they had been

170

working, and inside the general sketch there was a checking of many figures.

"What the dickens does it mean?" asked Sherry.

"It means that I've been searching through old Wilton's room," answered Lang. "And finally I found this in his private desk."

"That desk is locked. How could you get into it?"

"How did somebody get in there before me?" asked Lang with a snap.

"Great guns, man, do you accuse me? What would I be doing in his desk? And how could I possibly get into it unless I knew the way to find the key of it?"

Lang said at last, after a glare of hostility: "You're right, old son. I'm wrong. I've almost had an idea that you were sort of working for yourself on the side, in this here case, but I'm wrong. I'm glad of it!"

He leaned a heavy hand upon Sherry's shoulder.

"I'm about beat, Tiny," he declared. "It ought to be here! It ought to be here!"

"What?"

"The pearls, you doddering idiot!"

"Is that it? Is that what you've got there?"

"Well, I don't know," said Lang. "But that's my hunch. I think that I've put my hand on the key to the whole little mystery. I hope so, anyway!"

"If we got them—then we could get what poor Beatrice Wilton needs—the finest lawyer in the country."

"Aye, and that's why he's hunting so hard for them, too!"

"Who? For the pearls?"

"He's seen this paper," said the other with assurance. "He's seen it in the desk. I found this sheet on top of the pile yesterday. Somebody has been in Wilton's room looking the things over!"

"Layman, then, by gravy!" cried Sherry.

"Layman?" echoed Lang, and laughed with excitement. "I tell you, me son, that the gent that looked at that paper and opened the desk is also the gent that murdered Wilton!"

"The deuce! What brings you to that?"

171

"I don't know! I can't tell you all the steps."

"And, after all," cried Sherry suddenly, "why shouldn't Layman be the man? Why shouldn't Layman have murdered Wilton?"

"Him?" frowned Lang. "What would he have to gain by it?"

"Why—everything, if you'll stop to think of it! He was engaged to Beatrice Wilton, eh?"

"So they say."

"And if he married her, naturally he'd get his hands on her property."

"That's true. Yes. Go on."

"It stood to his interest to see that the year didn't elapse and Wilton come into guardianship over Beatrice Wilton. Great Lord, why haven't I thought of this before! The doctor, Lang. He's the man to think about! The doctor! I never even suspected him before! His interest to find the pearls, too, naturally; anyone's interest to find 'em! And who so apt to have access to this office as the doctor, too? I tell you, Pete, he's the killer. I wish to heaven that my brain were a little truer, and I'd prove it to you!"

Lang regarded him dubiously, like a man more than half persuaded, but at length he shook his head with decision.

"The doctor?" he said. "No, it's Fennel who did the job. Either Fennel and the girl, or Fennel alone!"

"Fennel? I almost forgot about him, since he disappeared."

"Of course you did! Fennel wanted to be forgotten. That's why he played such an open part at the first. He had a purpose in living at the hotel, d'you see? He had that all planned!"

"Come, come!" exclaimed Sherry. "I won't admit that. That's a little deep for me."

"Fennel lived at the hotel, pretended to be a drunk, and talked a lot and very loud about how much he knew about Wilton, didn't he?"

"That's true."

172

"Then one day he walks up the hill, meets Wilton, and murders him!"

"I see that."

"Either he's a deep, smart gent, or else the girl supplies the brains and tells him what to do," suggested Lang.

"She? Pete, she had nothing to do with it!"

"You don't believe what you say, yourself, so why try to tell me what you don't think, man?"

Sherry sighed. "She? Well, get back to Fennel. What do you think he was?"

"Faker, of course. You proved that, when you discovered the whiskey stains under the drain from the roof. You'll find that he was faked all the way through. Disguised, I mean. That's why he made such a public play and show of himself. He wanted to fix the wrong face in the eyes of the public. Then he'd just walk off and change, and be another man!"

"That would take a deep schemer!"

"And this is a deep job," declared Pete Lang, "because I'll tell you what: The girl has all the brains that anybody needs, and she'd play deep to have this job done according to the way she wants!"

"She did it? She planned and hired it?" cried Sherry.

"Go away and don't bother me," pleaded Lang. "I gotta think!"

CHAPTER THIRTY-TWO

THE TRIAL opened the next day with a great crowd in Clayrock. The courtroom was filled. But Sherry, for one, did not care to be there. Instead, he preferred to walk about the streets of the town, talking here and there, for he remembered what Beatrice Wilton had told him the evening before—that prejudice was so strong against her in the county that no jury could be found which would not have adjudged her guilty before they foregathered in the jury box.

That statement of hers he wanted to prove, now. And it was hard for him to believe. Western men were not like that.

He tried to fall into conversation on the subject half a dozen times until at last a man said to him bluntly: "Why d'you ask me what I think, Sherry? Everybody knows that you're for the girl. Well, what's the good of arguing about it?"

He had to wait until almost noon before he found an impartial listener, an oldish tough-looking mountaineer who regarded him with an unknowing eye, and with him Sherry, rejoiced, fell into talk.

"What'll happen to Beatrice Wilton?"

"I'll tell you what ought to happen," said the veteran.

"Well, tell me that."

"She had oughta hang!"

Sherry looked down to the ground and made a cigarette to cover his emotion.

"I've heard others guess that," said he. "I don't see why."

"You don't? It looks pretty clear to me!"

"Still I don't follow you. Why shouldn't it have been Fennel that did the killing?"

"That was the sailor drunk, eh? I tell you, if he had had anything to do with the case, the sheriff certainly would have had him a long time ago, wouldn't he?"

"I don't know that he would," said Sherry.

"And when did he ever miss?" asked the mountaineer aggressively.

Sherry was silent. There must have been failures, but he could not remember any. After all, the sheriff was apparently like a universal medicine, in the eyes of the men of his county. He could not fail to do what was right!

174

"I don't know," said Sherry at last. "But I suppose everybody makes mistakes now and then."

"Not Herb Moon," said the mountaineer. "He lives to do what's right, and he always does it. He don't live for nothing else!"

"But suppose he should be mistaken this one time —and get the girl hanged?"

"Serve her right," said the other. "These rich folks, they're all crooked. Never knowed one that wasn't! What's she? Why's a woman to be favored over a man? Murder's murder, ain't it?"

"I suppose it is. That doesn't prove her guilty."

"Young feller," said the old man, flushing with anger. "Don't set yourself up to be better and wiser than Herb Moon. There's others that have tried to do it, and they've always had a fall."

"I don't set myself up to be better and wiser. I say that the girl ought to have a fair chance."

"She'll get as fair a chance as she deserves. But look at the way that she's been carrying on—hiring a bully to run her enemies out of town! Makin' sure that nobody would be in the jury that would dare to vote agin' her!"

"Who do you mean?"

"I mean the great gun fighter, Sherry. If she'd hire a killer like that, what wouldn't she do? Murder? Murder ain't nothing to rich people!"

"I don't see that Sherry has been hired to run her enemies out of town."

"Ain't he for her?"

"I've heard that he is."

"Ain't he a gun fighter?"

"I don't think so."

"You don't think so! Young feller, your thinking is all crooked! Didn't Sherry take a show-down out of Fannie Slade and make him take water? Could anything less than a clever one have done that, I ask you?"

"And the girl's guilty because she has Sherry for a friend?" asked the big man, bitterly.

"The sheriff's against her, isn't he?"

"Yes, I suppose he is. He's refused her the legal rights that belong to her."

"Legal be darned," declared the other with heat. "What's right in the eye of the sheriff is right enough to suit me. And who he thinks guilty, I'm willin' to think guilty. If he makes a mistake, I'll make one, too! There ain't a wiser or a finer man on earth than Herb Moon. That's what I'm here to state!"

He had worked himself up into a fine frenzy, at this point, when a bystander took him by the arm and drew him away. What the newcomer said in a whisper could easily be guessed, for the old man, with a gasp, started off hastily down the street, glancing now and again back over his shoulder, as though he feared that Sherry, like some form out of a nightmare, might pursue him.

There was no such thought in Sherry's mind, however. He had proved amply that Beatrice Wilton was right, and that the attitude of the sheriff had so thoroughly poisoned all minds in the county that an impartial jury could not very well be picked.

Beatrice Wilton was lost!

Sherry went back to lunch at the hotel and found himself regarded gloomily and askance. He could understand why he was considered to be the hired retainer of a losing game, and the more formidable he was, the more unpopular! But he learned at the luncheon table that in one morning's work the jury had been selected, and that very afternoon testimony would begin to be taken.

He went toward the courtroom down-headed, filled with thought. He had prepared his tools days before. He had prepared his scheme, also. Immediately adjoining the jail, so close to it that a man could hardly walk down the path which separated the two buildings, was an empty house, and if there were a cellar of any size in the place, he should be able to dig through and beneath the foundations of the jail, and cut a tunnel upward. That done, he still would have to force a way

176

through the floor of the jail, and to do this in silence would probably be impossible.

He had determined on using blunt force. A charge of dynamite would open the floor. Once in the jail, another blast of dynamite would shatter the lock on the girl's cell. And, if she stubbornly refused to come with him, he could take her by force. Lang would be waiting with three horses of the best in the rear of the vacant house. And once in the saddle, Heaven send good luck to them and bad luck to Sheriff Herbert Moon.

Sherry by no means looked upon the task as a simple one And he knew perfectly well that that grim-faced jailer would be the very man to fight to the death to retain the prisoners who were under his charge. Furthermore, the people of Clayrock were a hardy lot. Once embarked on his task, it would mean a pair of well-oiled Colts in action from the first, but Sherry, gloomily adding up the result, determined on the work.

He diverged from the straight course toward the court in order to pass the jail, and doing so, to see again the vacant house. There it was, weatherbeaten, dilapidated, with the "To rent" shingle projecting from its front. But as Sherry came by, he saw a man seated in the wide-open doorway with a rifle leaning against the door jamb beside him.

"Hello!" said Sherry. "House rented at last?"

"Not rented. Occupied!" said the rifleman. And he patted his gun with a fond hand, and grinned at Sherry with a great deal of meaning.

The big man went on with a slower step.

It was, somehow, the most signal proof he had run across of the omniscient brain of the sheriff!

For he had no doubt that Herbert Moon had taken possession of the house for the very purpose of securing the last approach to the jail itself! And, going on past the wall of the jail, he noted its solidity, its depth, as signified by the frowning depths of the dark windows. It looked like a veritable fortress of the law. And he, single-handed, would have a wretched task in storming it.

He knew that Lang would follow him far, but he also knew that the cowpuncher never would commit himself to such a desperate act for the sake of a woman whom he already believed to be deeply implicated in the murder. Whatever was to be done, must be done by Sherry in person.

So, marching slowly past the front door of the jail, he regarded the door itself. It was ponderous, iron-clasped, and iron-bolted within, as he had observed on the preceding day. Yet a powerful charge of powder would doubtless smash it in, and once inside—

Well, it seemed more desperate than the plan of attack from beneath the building, but after all, the most desperate measures sometimes meet with the greatest success!

Little Herbert Moon came down the steps of the jail at that moment and nodded cheerfully at Sherry.

"You had your interview?" he asked.

"I did," said Sherry sadly.

"There's spirit in that girl," declared the sheriff. "A confounded lot of spirit, of course. And I admire her for it. But, at the same time, the law has to take its way. At the worst, it won't be the rope, Sherry, and ten or fifteen years of model conduct in the prison ought to give her a fair chance of a pardon from the governor. Western men are fair enough to women, you know!"

"Except you, Moon!" exclaimed Sherry in wrath. "Except you, man. You hate her as if she were a fiend! Will you tell me that I'm wrong?"

"If she murdered Wilton," said the sheriff, "does she deserve anything but hate?" Then he added smoothly: "If you want to see me again, one of these days, you'll always find me down here at the jail."

"Nearly living here?"

"Living here in fact—day and night. When I have a prisoner as beautiful as Beatrice Wilton—why, of course I have to take the best and most special care of her! You'll understand that, my lad!"

And Sherry turned away toward the court with

despair. The last hope had been stripped from his mind. For he knew that he never could force his way into the jail while the sheriff remained there on guard.

CHAPTER THIRTY-THREE

TO SHERRY all that passed in the next few days had the unreality and the horror of a nightmare, for he saw Beatrice Wilton being pressed irresistibly toward condemnation by judge and jury. And in the meantime it appeared to Sherry as though the entire country were licking its lips with horrid pleasure. Clayrock literally was filled with the clicking of cameras; and in the hot, stuffy courtroom, day by day, scores of eyes stared in morbid interest at the prisoner.

She bore herself very well in one respect and very badly in another. She was as calm and cool as stone; on the stand, her voice had tremors; she looked at the other witnesses for and against her without a frown or a smile; and she never appeared perturbed by anything that was put forward in evidence. This bearing of hers gave a good deal of dignity and importance to her case, but it practically destroyed her.

Two young lawyers worked out her side of the argument, and against them was the hard-headed district attorney. He had ways of violence, almost instinctively, because he was accustomed to deal with male criminals of the worst sort. To the bludgeoning of his rough assaults, the counsel of Beatrice Wilton begged her to oppose a feminine delicacy. If she would only be overcome, or appear to be overcome, by the brutality of the opposition, it might well be that she could win the sympathy of the jury. But she refused to make concessions of any kind. She remained erect in her chair, unflinching, calm, while the district attorney heaped upon her all the abuse of implication which declared her to be a cold-minded murderess, relentless, cruel, stern as a man. And, while he made these points in cross-examination, he seemed to be pointing to her, again and again, as though saying to the jury: "Notice this! She never flinches. The woman is a perfect monster!"

As for the defense, there was only one hope, and that was to establish Fennel as a sinister figure, a man who obviously intended to work some harm to Wilton from the moment he came to Clayrock, and who eventually succeeded in murdering his man.

To do that, they called upon Sherry and worked up his testimony as brightly as possible. It appeared through him that Fennel was an obvious sham. That his pretended drunkenness had been assumed for some ulterior purpose. That he was probably not a sailor at all. And certainly this man with the sinister intention had come to Wilton, had been walking with him at the moment of the murder. What folly, then, to imagine that such a woman as Beatrice Wilton deserved any share of the guilt when Fennel was not as yet detected or trailed? Why should the law seize upon the lamb instead of the wolf, simply because the lamb was nearest at hand?

But the cross-examination of the district attorney was terribly damaging. If Sherry was the star witness for the defense, he also turned out to be the star witness for the prosecution. He had to relate in detail how he had run in pursuit, had found Beatrice cowering, had been forced to carry her back to the place of the crime! And all this evidence had to be wrung from a most manifestly reluctant witness, who stood with his great fists balled, and a glare in his eyes, and perspiration streaking down his face.

"Look!" said the district attorney, with inexcusable brutality. "The man sees what his words are doing. He cannot help but understand that he is destroying the case of the woman he would give his life to assist. There, gentlemen of the jury, is a picture of misery and of—"

Here the judge stopped the peroration but it had had its effect. Sherry stood down from the witness stand, at last, perfectly confident that he had beaten to the ground the last hope of Beatrice Wilton, and he fixed upon her an eye of agony as he went out.

She, for her part, turned in her chair and nodded and smiled toward him with such sweetness that it stopped him like a blow. He went on unsteadily.

He heard voices on either side of him, muttering. He could not help but hear one woman say: "Poor fellow! He loves her, you see. I'm sorry for him, but not for that cold-blooded little minx!"

Sherry went out into the open air; Doctor Eustace Layman came out and stood beside him. The doctor was always present at every moment of the trial. He had a chair comparatively close to the two young lawyers who were defending Beatrice, and from time to time, as thoughts for the conduct of the case occurred to him, he scribbled notes and passed them across to the legal hands.

As the trial continued, Sherry's respect for the doctor increased enormously. For one thing, there was no pretense or sham about him. He never paraded his feelings. He never obtruded upon anyone the knowledge that this girl was his betrothed. But, keeping as cool and as quiet as Beatrice Wilton herself, he gave his whole energy of mind to helping where he could.

"I think I've sent her to prison for life," said Sherry bluntly.

And suddenly the other astonished him by saying: "And suppose the sheriff is right, after all, and you and I are wrong, Sherry?"

The big man turned to him in bewilderment.

"You and I are the only people in the entire world who think she's innocent," added the doctor. And then he concluded: "But it never makes any real difference to a man. He believes what he wants to believe, and that's true of you and of me, eh?"

Sherry went off up the street; the doctor went the other way. The court had adjourned, and Sherry relieved his feelings by taking his horse and riding furiously off into the country, never turning back for the Wilton house until his animal was wet with sweat. Then, with creaking saddle leather, he climbed the clay rock and put up his mustang in the stable.

When he came to the front of the house, he stopped, shocked. Up the steps to Wilton's entrance went a thin streak of crimson. Before the door, it widened to a little pool.

Blood!

He went in hurriedly, and followed the same trail, with growing horror, to his own room. He found the door locked, and in answer to the wrangling of his hand upon the knob a voice which he barely recognized as that of Lang called to him: "Sherry?"

"Yes," he answered.

Then: "Wait—I'll unlock the door!"

There was a faint sound of fumbling, then the lock turned, and Sherry pushed into the chamber. Lang had collapsed upon a bunk. He was stripped to the waist, and a great bandage made of a sheet was wound around his middle. It was much stained with blood, as was everything in the room!

"Great Scott!" cried Sherry, "What's happened, man?"

"Fennel!" said Lang faintly. "I'm cooked, and Fennel did it!"

He lay flat on the bunk, breathing with difficulty. The sheet had been drawn so tight that his chest heaved with every inspiration.

"Let me have a look at that—he shot you!" exclaimed Sherry.

"There's no good looking," said Lang faintly. "I'm about done, old man. I think I always had an idea that I'd get my finish in this dirty work. You wanted it—Sherry!"

182

The big man groaned.

"Let me talk," said Lang. "You know the drawing that I found in the room of Wilton's? I guessed that it was the plan for the hiding place where he'd put the pearls. I missed it when I went out with you. Today I looked it over again and finally I had my inspiration. I went out to the same clearing, and worked everything by reverse. The very first whack of the pick, it clinked on metal. I dragged up a little copper box. Opened it up. It was filled to the brim with pearls, man! And while I was looking, I got this through the back!"

He paused, breathing again with difficulty.

"I fell on my face," he went on, "but I pulled my gun as I was going down. I managed to twist around, and I had a glimpse of Fennel getting ready to shoot again—and his face looked like—like a man that had been living like a beast out here in the woods. Why, he's been hiding in these here bad lands all the time!"

"Waiting for someone to begin a hunt for the stuff that he couldn't find?" suggested Sherry.

"That's it! I'm getting wabbly in the head. Like a newborn calf, old son. Listen hard! I swung my gun around on Fennel and, instead of risking another shot, he slipped away through the trees. Then I took the box and started back for home. I had to crawl most of the way. Once I fainted. Thank Heaven, he didn't follow me close enough to find me then! I got here. Since then, I've been waitin' for you, prayin' for you —and dyin' like a dog, old man!"

"You've talked enough," declared Sherry. "Keep the rest of your wind. I'm going to have you out of this, Pete. I dragged you into it. You never liked the business. And now—"

"Steady, steady," said Pete Lang. "I'm not going to last many more minutes. I wanted to last long enough to tell you who Fennel most likely is. It'll give even you a shock. This here gent that played drunken sailor and all the rest is nobody but—"

He had raised himself a little upon one elbow, in his excitement, and now he interrupted himself with a faint gasp, and his staring eyes went past Sherry to the open doorway. There was a puffing, hissing sound; a heavy spat of a bullet piercing bone, and Pete Lang sank back on the bunk, dead.

Sherry had whirled the instant he heard the sound, and, whirling, he had both guns in his hands.

In the distance, close to the front door of the house, he had a glimpse of that never-to-be-forgotten face of Fennel, shrouded almost to the eyes with matted hair.

The front door was jerked open. Sherry fired as Fennel sprang through. Then, as he leaped in pursuit, heard the the lock turn. He threw his whole weight against the door. It was perfectly solid and threw him back, half stunned.

A light, quick step struck the steps and then crunched on the gravel of the path, and he knew that Fennel was gone once more from his ken.

He went slowly, sick at heart, to the death room, and there he leaned gloomily above the body of his dead friend.

Who was Fennel? The question could not be answered by the calmly smiling lips of Pete Lang, who lay with a certain air of triumph, as it seemed to Sherry, one hand spread out over the copper box beside him, for which he had given his life.

CHAPTER THIRTY-FOUR

PETE LANG was gone, and the last testimony of the work he had done lay under the dead man's hand. Sherry took up the box and opened it with a sense of loathing. But the loathing disappeared at the first glance. The little box was filled to the brim with creamy light. He sifted it through his fingers, and it showered back in a beautiful rain into the box. Was it not for the sake of this box that three men already had died—Wilton, Capper, Pete Lang?

Perhaps he himself would be the fourth.

And a sort of superstitious horror possessed Sherry. Whatever he did, he would not keep that treasure in his possession. He took the box under his arm, settled his hat on his head, and started straight down the hill.

Coming out of the garden to the street below, he encountered Doctor Eustace Layman, coming up with his usual brisk, light stride. He nodded cheerfully at Sherry.

"This hill is put here for our sins," said the doctor.

"How is Miss Wilton?" asked Sherry.

"She? As well as can be expected, as they say. She knows, now."

"That the case will go against her?"

"Yes."

"After I'd testified. Of course it was what I said that turned the trick."

"And what difference did it make?" asked Layman. "The sheriff already knew what you had to say. They could have had it out of him on the stand, if they'd wished. By Jove, you've cut your hand, Sherry!"

Sherry looked down and saw the crimson on his fingers.

"My hand isn't cut," said he.

"And what in the world has happened, Sherry?"

"Lang has been murdered by Fennel—after he found the pearls!"

"Good Heavens! Lang murdered! Fennel? Fennel, did you say? Do you mean that, Sherry?"

"I saw his cursed face," said Sherry bitterly.

The doctor grew greatly excited.

"I want to follow this clearly. Lang killed by Fennel. You saw the brute do it! Lang—after he'd found the pearls! And Fennel murdered him and stole the jewels and—"

185

"He didn't steal them. They're under my arm in this box, just now."

"The pearls?"

"Yes."

"My head spins, Sherry. Lang dead—Fennel— Poor Lang! There was a brave, honest fellow. A little sour, but brave as they come. But do you see what this horrible affair means for Beatrice?"

"For her?" asked Sherry dully.

"It means that she'll get off scot free! Don't you understand? It's like a stroke of luck. This second murder practically proves that Fennel committed the first one. Isn't that clear as day?"

"Ah," sighed the big man. "I hadn't thought of that! I hadn't thought of that!" And suddenly he lifted his fallen head. "The life of poor Pete to save her!" he groaned.

"But even if that weren't the case, you have a fortune under your arm there, man," cried Layman. "With a hundredth part of it, you can save her. You can bring in a great lawyer who will soon tangle up this affair so completely that the district attorney and that prejudiced judge won't know where they're standing!"

"Use part of this?" asked Sherry. "I couldn't touch it. It goes to the sheriff, now. It's nothing of mine!"

The doctor stepped a little back from him, angry and surprised.

"I didn't understand," he said with some bitterness. "I thought that you really wanted her to win out!"

"Did you?" murmured Sherry. "And am I to steal to do it? Lang has died for her. I think that's enough. His blood against hers. I'm going on, Layman."

He turned and strode past the doctor, and went hurrying down into the hot street of the city.

He went to the jail, and there he found the sheriff.

He was not easily admitted. As he went in to interview Herbert Moon, two armed men stood in the doorway behind him. Sherry looked upon them with a vague smile.

"I'm not dangerous," said he to the sheriff. "My

186

teeth have been pulled for today, Moon! Will you send those fellows away?"

The sheriff, instead of answering, looked steadily at the stained hands of the giant.

"It's the blood of Pete Lang," said Sherry. "Fennel killed him today."

The sheriff leaped from his chair.

"Fennel again! He wouldn't dare again!" exclaimed Herbert Moon.

"Fennel has killed Pete Lang, I saw him with my own eyes. And this is why Pete was shot in the first place."

He lifted the lid of the box of pearls. The sheriff dipped his hand into them, and let a rain of them fall back. Then he waved the two guards from the doorway.

"I brought it in to you," said Sherry, "because I think that this ought to be enough to free Beatrice Wilton."

The sheriff opened a small safe which stood in a corner of the office and into it he thrust the box and its treasure.

"This goes a little beyond me!" he murmured. "I expected almost anything, but not quite this!"

He was pale with emotion.

"And she's cleared?" insisted Sherry.

"Beatrice Wilton?"

"Yes."

"In what way?" asked the sheriff, frowning.

"I'm not an expert in these affairs. But when the jury knows that Fennel has been seen to commit another murder, won't they be apt to put the burden of the first one on him?"

"Do you think so?"

"I do."

"You're wrong," answered the sheriff. "After today in the courtroom, I don't think there's a chance to defend her. Perhaps I haven't a right to say that, but I've always wanted to be frank with you, Sherry."

Sherry flushed darkly.

"You know law," he admitted, "but I have an idea that we don't pay and get nothing in the world. Lang died for that girl, Moon. And by George, you'll see that he didn't die in vain for her."

"Do you know the story of these pearls?" asked the sheriff suddenly.

"I've heard it. You'll hear it yourself, before very long."

"From whom?"

"Two sailors——"

"The ones who asked to see Fennel's outfit?"

"That's right."

"The coroner again," said the sheriff, to himself. "The third time in the same house! Both the Wiltons. Now this cowpuncher! Sherry, will you ride up the hill with me! If I can't bring justice home in this case, I've reached the end of my rope and leave my office! I'm an old man, Sherry, and my brain is weakening."

"You?" exclaimed Sherry. "There's no other man in the world who thinks so."

"Bah!" snarled Herbert Moon savagely. "Do you hear me? If I'd acted quicker, done as I felt I should have done long ago, your friend Pete Lang would be alive at this moment."

He went to the wall, picked his hat from a peg and jammed it down upon his head.

Sherry was still staring after this last statement.

"What did you know? What should you have done?" he asked earnestly.

The sheriff hesitated.

"You've seen this case from the beginning?" he said at last.

"I didn't see the death of Everett Wilton," said Sherry.

"That's true, that's true! But even without that, haven't you been able to guess?"

"That Beatrice Wilton is the cause of all this?"

"The cause? I never called her the cause! A tool is not a cause, man. An instrument is not a cause of a murder!"

He took Sherry suddenly by the arm.

"Let's get away from this building. I hate walls. I

188

loathe brick and stone set up in courses. Sometimes I think that what we speak inside a room remains there like a thought floating in the air, and the next person who comes in will be able to read it. Heaven forgive if my thought should be read! It would be ruin to a great cause, young man!"

It occurred to Sherry that, after all, there might be something in what the sheriff had said about advancing years. Certainly, he had been talking in a very odd manner.

They went out onto the street together.

"You have friends in Clayrock," said the sheriff.

"I? Not a one!"

"Ah, but you have. You have more friends here then you think. They admire Lew Sherry. They admire his size and his strength, and his straight shooting. They admire the man who broke down Fannie Slade, at the last. You have plenty of friends, though they hold off for a time, while you're mixed up in this murder mystery. But today or tomorrow you might meet some friendly spirits here in Clayrock, Sherry. Do you understand what I mean?"

"I don't," he admitted frankly. "What you've been saying sounds a little bit queerer than anything any man ever has said to me before."

"I suppose it does," said Moon. "But I'll be franker. I want to tell you that if a syllable of what I've said to you in the last few moments gets abroad, it will undo a great work for me!"

"The conviction of Beatrice Wilton," scowled Sherry.

The sheriff turned upon him impatiently.

"I give you my word that she's not even in my mind at this moment. I'm thinking of bigger quarry!"

"And what do you want me to do?"

"Give me a solemn promise that you'll keep your mouth shut about what I've said to you!"

"I will," said Sherry, "because I don't understand a word that you've spoken!"

189

CHAPTER THIRTY-FIVE

THE TRIAL lasted four days. The case went to the jury at noon of that day, and thirty minutes later the jury filed back into the box to give its verdict.

All of Clayrock was there, or as much of Clayrock as could be squeezed into the room. Every window was blocked with heads. The door was beset by a solidly wedged mob of at least a hundred persons, and in the midst of a tense silence, the foreman pronounced "Guilty!" and a long, shuddering sigh went through the audience.

Sherry had been expecting the blow with such perfect certainty that he had armed himself against the shock, and now he turned his gloomy gaze upon his companions in the court.

He noted, particularly, the gleaming eyes which the women fixed upon Beatrice Wilton, and the proud head of Beatrice herself, sustaining this burden which had been dropped upon her spirit. He saw familiar heads, here and there—the bartender from the hotel, agape, his brutal face vaguely smiling as he drank in the sensation; the sheriff on one of the front benches, at the side, strangely, of Doctor Eustace Layman.

And, above all, he noted that one of the young lawyers who had fought out the case for Beatrice, now turned and murmured something to his associate, and they both chuckled together.

A piece of callousness that made the blood of Sherry run cold!

Voices mumbled. He saw Beatrice Wilton led out and standing before the judge, a man guarding her upon either side. He heard the judge demanding if she had anything to say why sentence should not be pronounced upon her, and then there began a sharp scuffling at the rear of the courtroom, and voices clamoring in high tones. The judge rapped angrily for order. His most solemn moment in many years of law was being spoiled.

Then one of Beatrice Wilton's lawyers—Craven was his name—started a little forward from his chair.

"Your Honor," he said, "there is nothing that my client can say except that she is innocent. We have been waiting for several days, however, in the hope of something more. That hope is now fulfilled. Your Honor, the disturbance from the back of the room comes from two witnesses who have just arrived from a long journey. Their testimony will prove that Beatrice Wilton is totally innocent, and it will place the whole burden of the crime definitely upon the shoulders of Fennel, the slayer of Peter Lang! Will you reopen the case and let me put them on the stand?"

Had the judge been the most formal official in the world, he could not have resisted the vast stir of excitement which troubled the courtroom.

Way was made. Up the courtroom aisle came two swaggering individuals, walking as though to the sway of a deck—one tall and one short—Bud Arthur and his bunkie, Jerry!

Sherry looked upon them with a vague hope of he knew not what! They were brought to the witness bench. Bud Arthur was sworn in. The jury sat tense in its jury box. The judge himself was tingling with excitement, and ghostly whispers passed through the crowd.

Young Craven, like a skipper who loves a storm wind, stood in the court and smiled from side to side.

"Your Honor," said he, "we intend to liberate Miss Wilton. In her place we shall put the real criminal. He is now in the courtroom!"

Even the spectacular entrance of Jerry and Bud was as nothing compared with the sensation which followed at this point.

"We have had one member of this pair ready since last night," went on the lawyer. "But we have been waiting for the arrival of the second man, who——"

Here the district attorney sprang up with an impassioned objection. The judge, like one tired of the formalities of the law, simply raised his hand.

"Sit down, Charlie," said he. "We've had a good many days condemning this young woman; and now if there's anything to be said in her defense, I'm going to hear it, no matter how it's put before us!"

At this, the crowd roared with applause. The jury grinned and grunted with agreement. The suspicion and dislike which had surrounded Beatrice Wilton these many days was dissolved at a stroke.

"Mr. Arthur," said the young Mr. Craven, "what is your employment?"

"Sailor."

"And what brought you to Clayrock?"

"To get what was coming to me."

"From what? Coming to you from what?"

"My share of the pearls that Captain Oliver Wilton had swiped down in the Sulus."

The shock of this statement fairly stunned the crowd. Beatrice Wilton looked keenly across at her lawyer, and he nodded to her. As much as to say that he was sorry that he had had to keep her so long in the dark, but soon he would make all things clear.

"We will follow you after that. You came to Clayrock to see Mr. Wilton?"

"Yes."

"Did you see him?"

"Not quite. He was dead."

"What did you do?"

"Hung around the pawnshops. We figgered that if Wilton was dead, somebody else would have the stuff. They'd likely pawn some of it for ready money. That's what happened. Lew Sherry, he pawned a pearl."

There was a deep rumbling at this. People next to Sherry shrank away from him. Someone called out

192

loudly: "If Sherry's the murderer, he ought to be taken in hand. The man's dangerous!"

"My dear friends," said the lawyer, addressing the crowd with a total lack of court etiquette, "Lew Sherry had nothing whatever to do with the murders, as you'll shortly understand. But there is another man in this courtroom who is now trembling in his boots, though he puts a brave face upon it. Mr. Arthur, you saw a pearl pawned?"

"Yes, I seen Sherry pawn it. I was watching that shop for three days! I trailed him. I'd heard about him before. Me and my partner, Jerry, come up to the Wilton garden, and there we cornered Pete Lang all alone. We figgered that if Sherry knew where the stuff was, Lang would know. We cornered Lang. We had him with his hands up, when Sherry took us from behind and turned the tables complete! He got us helpless. A pair of guns in Sherry's hands is doggone discouraging!"

At this the crowd laughed, and the judge himself did not call for silence. Even the clerk, writing swiftly, paused to chuckle. Vast good humor possessed everyone. They were about to witness a kill, and they were content to see the race from the beginning.

"Sherry put us right," said Bud Arthur.

He stood up in his place.

"Do I get you wrong if I tell everything, Sherry?" he asked.

And the deeply booming voice of Sherry made answer: "Tell everything from the beginning, and tell it straight!"

There was another gasp of delight from the throng.

"Sherry let us know that when Wilton was found dead, Lang had got out of his pocket a handful of jewels and a piece of paper. That paper was a letter from Fennel, asking to see Wilton, and asking for his split of the loot. Lang and Sherry had held back that stuff, because the idea was that it showed that Fennel had gone to ask for pearls, and Wilton had taken out the share of Fennel to give to him. Lang and

193

Sherry, they were plumb anxious not to get Miss Wilton into any trouble!"

This naive statement brought a cheer from everyone except the judge, who beat upon his desk, but smiled even as he tried to frown.

"Sherry told me," went on Arthur, "that he had pawned one of those pearls, not for the sake of making money to blow, but to have enough funds to keep him and Lang going on the job, because he still hoped that he could do something for the girl. He showed us the rest of the pearls that they had, and he offered to split them with me and Jerry if we could help in the work. I didn't know how we could help, but Sherry said we should look over the stuff that Fennel had left behind him. We went down and done that."

"And what did you learn?" coached Craven, the lawyer.

"We seen that it come out of Cap Wendell's shop in San Pedro. It was just poor enough to suit him. It didn't look like a sailor's outfit, either. It was just faked up. There was two sizes of socks, for instance. One size would've fitted Miss Wilton. The other was big enough for Sherry!"

"Will you keep your witness to the point?" asked the judge good-naturedly, waving the district attorney back into his chair as that gentleman leaped up to make another legal assault.

"I'll do my best," smiled Craven. "And then what happened, Mr. Arthur?"

"We seen Sherry. He says: 'Go out to San Pedro and find out if Wendell remembers anything about the gent that bought the layout.'

"We done that as fast as the train would snake us along. We got to San Pedro and we walked into Cap Wendell's shop. 'Morning, boys,' says he. 'A bit of a blow they have been having off the coast, ain't they?' "

"Answer the questions that I put to you," commanded Craven.

"Yes, sir."

"Well then, you asked Wendell about the buyer of

the sea chest and its contents. You were able to identitfy them?"

"Sure," said Bud Arthur. "It ain't often that a seaman wants to buy a whole new outfit. Mostly, he's just filling in holes, here and there, where the swabs have cleaned him out on board ship. Wendell remembered this gent pretty well. He'd come in in ragged-looking clothes. He had a broad-brimmed hat pulled down over his face. Looked like he'd seen better days."

"What was his face like?"

"Wendell, he couldn't see it very clear at first. He got the gent to take off his hat, after a while though. Then he seen that he had a sizable, fine big bump of a forehead that made the rest of his face look small. And he had a kind of a bald head—balder than it should've been for his age, and his face was pretty pale and thin. And this here gent was pretty tall, and made sort of light and active, like he'd make a good hand for going aloft."

"Your Honor," said Craven to the judge, "may I take this witness off the stand, and put on another, at this point?"

He added: "I want to ask Doctor Eustace Layman what he was doing in San Pedro buying a sailor's outfit, under the name of Fennel!"

CHAPTER THIRTY-SIX

SO THE blow had fallen. And, to a man, the people of the courtroom arose.

They saw Sheriff Herbert Moon rising at the side of Eustace Layman, and they saw that in the hand of the sheriff there was a man-sized revolver which was pressed into the ribs of the doctor.

"Layman? Layman?" exclaimed the judge, bewildered.

And then, with a vast effort, he regathered the official dignity and calm—which, of course, never can be disturbed!

Doctor Layman was entirely calm.

"Do I understand that I am invited to take the witness stand?" he asked.

"That's what you can understand," said the sheriff. "With your permission, Your Honor, I'll search this gentleman, first."

"By what right do you presume to search me?" said the doctor as calmly as before.

"By the right of arrest," answered the sheriff, his manner equally polite, but firm.

"And for what crime am I arrested?" asked the doctor.

"For the murders of Oliver Wilton and Peter Lang," said the sheriff.

And then, out of the throat of Sherry, tormented with wonder, burst the cry: "Fennel! *That* is Fennel!"

For now he saw as with an inspired vision that the strangely shaped head of Fennel might well be the doctor's, that towering forehead masked with a wig of matted hair.

He saw that vision; to attempt to understand how the doctor could have played the double role was beyond him! He waited, tense and wondering.

The sheriff was "fanning" Layman, and producing a stub-nosed revolver from a hip pocket, and from beneath his left arm pit a long, slender gun with a peculiar attachment at the end of the muzzle. The veritable type of the .22-caliber revolver with the silencer which had destroyed Oliver Wilton and poor Peter Lang! There was a gasping intake of breath around the courtroom as this detail was noted. Even the judge sat rigid in his chair, and Eustace Layman grew pale and set of face.

Bud Arthur was taken from the stand; Layman replaced him.

The district attorney made a quick turn up and down the space before his chair and slumped heavily down into it.

Plainly he was taken aback!

The preliminaries of identification were quickly ended.

"Dr. Layman," said Craven, "fifteen days ago, did you or did you not go to the store of Wendell in San Pedro and buy the outfit which afterward appeared in the possession of the so-called Fennel in this town?"

The doctor gathered himself, hesitated—

"I cannot answer," he said, "without advice of counsel."

"Did you or did you not," roared Craven, apparently suddenly furious, "several months ago talk with the Chinese cook when you met him one evening in the woods back of the Wilton house, and did he tell you at that time that he had seen Oliver Wilton thrust his brother, Everett Wilton, over the edge of the cliff to fall down into the rush of the water below?"

"I believe," said the doctor, as cool as ever, "that you are trying to put a statement into my mouth. I decline to answer."

"Is it not true," said the eager young lawyer, "that you used this knowledge to blackmail Oliver Wilton, forcing him to admit you into his house, to place you constantly with his niece, and to encourage her engagement to you?"

The doctor said not a word. Everyone in the courtroom was leaning forward except Beatrice Wilton, who sat stunned and helpless with the shock of these strange new charges.

"Your Honor," said Craven, "we are going to attempt to demonstrate these charges. From the first, Sheriff Moon has suspected the truth about this case, but he has done all that he could to give no sign of his suspicions, for fear lest the bird fly from the cage. He has waited to the last moment, collecting proofs.

And the last proof has been furnished by the arrival of Arthur and his friend from San Pedro.

"I hope that we have already offered sufficient testimony to make it necessary to reopen this case. After that, I shall demonstrate that the sheriff's suspicions were absolutely correct. I am going to show by witnesses and by every reasonable inference that Doctor Eustace Layman is an adventurer. I am going to show you that there are other crimes in his past, though none as heinous as these. I am going to prove to you that he first forced himself upon Miss Wilton and made himself useful to her after the death of her father, until she permitted herself to be engaged to him. That he was contented with the arrangement only so long as he thought it would make him heir to the fortune of Everett Wilton; that when he learned that the control of this fortune was about to pass into the hands of Oliver Wilton he determined to do away with that man, and succeeded. That when Sherry and Lang, two brave and devoted men—"

A rushing murmur, like the sound of a storm, swept through the court, and then a loud roar of applause deafened Sherry. He looked about him, bewildered. Shining eyes were turned toward him. Hands smote his broad back. Words of approval and cheer greeted him!

Craven took more heart. The judge, as stunned as any witness in the case, could only stare and let the torrent of words flow on. Even the district attorney was helpless.

"When these two heroic men," went on Craven, "enlisted themselves in the service of Miss Wilton after the murder of her uncle, at first Doctor Layman was pleased enough to have their assistance. But then he discovered that Mr. Sherry was pushing close to a discovery of the true identity of the supposed Fennel. When he began to fear this, he determined to do away with Mr. Sherry. We are going to prove through the testimony of the notorious Fannie Slade, now in the hands of Sheriff Moon and held until this proper moment for testimony, that that man was hired by Layman to come to Clayrock and, together with his attendant bullies, hunt down and murder Sherry. We all know how that plot was foiled by the extraordinary daring of Mr. Sherry himself—"

Applause again; a thunderclap of rejoicing!

."Throughout, you will see that Mr. Sherry, always, was the block upon which the well-devised schemes of the doctor were wrecked. The sheriff was the first to realize this, dimly in the beginning. He continued to throw forward all possible evidence against Miss Wilton—it was the bait which kept in Clayrock this detestable murderer!"

Craven paused. Dead silence followed his last words. Baleful eyes glared at the doctor, and he, his pale face unmoved, looked grimly back at everyone without flinching.

"Then came the time," said Craven, "when Lang himself discovered that Fennel and the doctor were one! At last, he guessed it very strongly. He consulted the sheriff. The sheriff begged him to say nothing; to wait for a more opportune time. And in that manner, to the great grief of the sheriff and of all honest men, poor Lang became a martyr to the cause to which he and his friend had given themselves so freely. What are we to say, Your Honor, of men like these two, who fought for the sake of justice to a helpless girl?"

Now Beatrice Wilton had borne up against all the assaults of her apparent enemies, but at this public touch of sympathy, she melted into tears.

The judge himself was moved.

"Still," went on Craven, "it appeared that the doctor was going to have a fair chance of winning. He could not know the mind of the sheriff. He could not know of the trip that the two sailors had taken to San Pedro. He could not know that Wendell himself, responding to a telegram, has actually started from San Pedro, and will be in this courtroom at any moment to identify Eustace Layman as the false Fennel. This masquerader, this murderer with silent guns, this detestable scoundrel, to defend himself in case of need, actually suggested to Miss Wilton that she use the weapon and train herself with it as for her own defense at the time when the murder of her father enabled him to persuade her that her own life probably stood in great danger.

"That was his plan, and that was the plan which would have succeeded if it had not been for the combined efforts of our sheriff, and of Lewis Sherry. The woman who he was engaged to marry was, in case the law came down too hard upon his heels, to bear the danger of the charge. He did not want to lose her. But better that her life should be ruined than that his precious neck should be stretched! And then, having murdered Lang before that man could tell Sherry of his suspicions as to the real identity of the murderer, he attempted again, in the person of his proper self, to persuade Sherry to keep the pearls—of which you are to hear more later and in greater detail—and use them in hiring more efficient lawyers for the defense of Miss Wilton.

"Because he began to see, now, that it was unlikely that he could get his hands upon the Wilton fortune. The sheriff had blocked him there. From the very first, with apparent tyranny, he had managed to prevent Miss Wilton from seeing the doctor, or from conveying to the outside a single scrap of writing by means of which she could bestow upon him the right to draw checks on the bank in her name! Had that power been so conferred, you need have no doubt that the admirable doctor would soon have gathered in the entire estate, and then departed for other lands!"

He paused for breath, and then added:

"That, Your Honor, is the case which we will now attempt to prove. As for the clumsy defense which I have hitherto made for Miss Wilton, I ask her pardon and yours. My hands were tied. The terrible strain she has passed through has been the price which she had to pay for the sake of attempting to bring justice home to this double villain. A strain so terrible that she has been tempted to destroy herself, being in total despair. No amends can be made to her, really. But the first step will be, of course, to ask the jury to reconsider their verdict, and to declare her blameless, as she has been in every way from the first. And then justice on this cold-faced and secret murderer!

"I am going to develop to you, also, the story of an unfortunate man, Oliver Wilton—a good man who committed one crime, that spectacular raid upon the pearl fishery in the far-off Sulus. And because of that he was driven from evil to evil. He was forced to take the life of his brother, who was beginning to learn the truth about the loss of the *Princess Marie*. He was forced to make for himself a steel-lined room, because he knew that danger was on his heels. But one wise step he took, and that was to employ the man who could not save his own forfeited life, but who could bring justice down upon the arch criminal of all!"

CHAPTER THIRTY-SEVEN

HOW MANY typewriters purred furiously, writing down pages of copy; how many telegraphers clicked out the long columns of news; how many cameras snapped every detail over again—the courthouse; the court-room; the judge; the jury—smiling broadly, all twelve; the young lawyer; the cold face of Eustace Layman, ever calmly self-contained; the furious excitement of the crowd; Beatrice Wilton's wide eyes as she listened to the words which spelled her safety; the portrait of brave Peter Lang, murdered, repeated with a black border; and views of how the strong men of Clay-rock rose in their might and seized upon Lewis Sherry, and heaved him upon their shoulders in all his un-wieldly bulk, and bore him protesting and struggling from the courtroom, and paraded him through the streets of Clayrock, and elected him with a universal acclaim to the small brotherhood of honest men and heroes who can fight for a lost cause without hope of a reward.

But Sherry himself, a lonely man, sat at last in a room in the hotel, and gazed moodily out the window. He felt that he had been drenched in death and tragedy. Capper, Everett Wilton, Oliver Wilton, Peter Lang, had all been destroyed. And now, perhaps, the doctor's life would pay the final forfeit.

And yet not the sense of gloomy tragedy alone was sufficient to give him this feeling of an empty heart.

A tap came at the door. The sheriff stood before him. They clasped hands and looked long and gravely upon one another.

"I came to tell you that the last step has been taken," said the sheriff.

"Has he confessed?"

"By implication. Layman is dead."

"He killed himself?"

"He had resolution. You'll find a peculiar contempt for life among some doctors. This fellow found a long splinter of stone in his cell in the jail. He drove it into his temple and died instantly. The best way, I have no doubt. And yet, rather a foolish thing. There was only one really important clue, one fact against him: that he had bought the clothes in San Pedro which afterward appeared in the sea chest of Fennel."

Sherry sank again into thought.

"Now that the tangle is cleared away," said he, "I want to ask you why it is that you never attempted to arrest me for the killing of Capper?"

"Because I knew that you were not guilty."

"You knew that?"

"I'll show you the proof."

He took Sherry down to the room where, on that first memorable evening that had finally involved the cow-puncher in all this train of drama, he and Capper had been dragged, senseless. In the baseboard which ran around the room, he pointed out a deep hole.

"If you had shot Capper in a struggle, and the bullet had driven on through his head, it would have entered the wall at the height of a man. But, as a matter of fact, the bullet entered this baseboard."

"That is what Wilton told me, that I deliberately murdered the man in his sleep!"

"Did he tell you that? Of course, to get you under his thumb. You were the sort of a man he needed! Very well, but see the angle of this hole!" He placed a pencil in it. "To what does it point?"

"Toward the window."

"From the window came that shot. Mark the cunning of Wilton! He had stolen your revolver. He waited there outside the window for a time when you were rapidly regaining consciousness, because your bulk enabled you to throw off more quickly the effects of the drug which he, Wilton, had placed in your drink. As you rose to your knees, he fired through the window and killed Capper, and then he threw the revolver so that it landed at your feet."

Sherry stared.

"And then, sheriff, why didn't you arrest Wilton?"

"Because if I had, it would have ended my chance of dipping a good deal deeper into an important mystery. I could guess that Wilton wanted to get rid of Capper. Then it appeared that he needed a bodyguard against other dangers. What were those dangers? What had Wilton done? I was fumbling in the dark. And lives have been lost on account of my delay, I know. But there is only one that I regret—Lang. The memory of that man will never be out of my head. As for the others—Everett Wilton was killed before I so much as suspected the murderer. Oliver Wilton, Layman, Fennel, Capper, were all rascals, of course. I'd like to use a gentler name for Oliver Wilton. But, after all, he was a murderer. And as for Lang, I have one consolation—that he died doing his duty, like a brave man. We don't sorrow a great deal for men who die on battlefields for their country, Sherry. Why should we feel differently about the heroes of peace, who haven't brass bands to urge them on and medals to reward them?"

"You've done a great thing in this case," said Sherry.

"I was a man standing in the dark, waiting for a light," replied the sheriff. "You brought me the light, old man, when you sent that pair of sailors to San Pedro. Miss Wilton has given them so much money that they won't be sober the rest of their lives; and when they've spent it, they know that they can come back to her for more! What a woman, Sherry! What a heart, and what a soul!"

"Is she steadier?" asked Sherry.

"As steady as a rock. She wants to see you."

"I'm starting back for the range," said Sherry hastily.

"Why?"

"Where I can find enough fresh air to blow this trouble out of my brain!"

"Are you starting at once?"

"Yes."

"Without even seeing her, man?"

"I'll send her a note," said Sherry.

"You won't have to do that."

"No?"

"Because," said the sheriff, "I had an idea that you would be exactly such a fool as this! And I suggested that she'd better come down here to the hotel to find you."

Sherry started up.

"The dickens you did!" said he.

And here came a light, light tap at the door.

The sheriff opened it.

He said: "I was right. The young fool was about to run away. Perhaps you can talk him into better sense. I'm going down to get a drink. I think I need one."

"But—wait one instant—sheriff—" stammered Beatrice Wilton.

"I'll be back before you know it," said the sheriff, and resolutely closed the door behind him.

And then they heard the lock click.

Sherry strode to it and shook the knob.

"Confound him!" said he. "He's locked the door."

She hurried to the window and looked anxiously down, almost as though she were contemplating an escape in that direction.

Then they turned and slowly faced one another.

"You were leaving Clayrock?" she asked with a sort of cold politeness.

"I was," answered Sherry bluntly.

"Without giving me a chance to see you?"

"I know," said Sherry. "You wanted to thank me, of course. But—to tell the truth, I didn't want thanks!"

He let a ring of emotion get into a part of that sentence, and bit his lip afterward, ashamed of it.

"There's the business side of it, then," said the girl.

"Yes?"

"I mean to say, that my uncle had offered you a thousand dollars a day. For ten days. And now there's no reason under the sun why you shouldn't take the money."

"Money!" said Sherry, half choked. "Money? For me?"

Then, as she looked at him, half frightened, he added: "There's Lang. He has an invalid brother somewhere. You could pay that money to him."

"I shall do it! And take care of the poor man, besides! Poor Peter Lang! Poor Peter Lang!"

Then she added:

"Is there simply nothing that you'll let me do for you?"

"For me?" There's nothing that I need. There's nothing that I want," answered Sherry. "I'm going back to the range, right away. That's the place for me; I never was meant for a life in a town, you see."

She looked at him with a sort of despair.

"I think it's hardly fair and kind to me," said she. "You go away and leave me in terrible debt to you!"

"I don't want to bother you. You see, there's nothing that I need."

"Nothing?"

"No."

She looked down at the floor, and then forced her eyes to meet his.

"There's nothing you could ask of me that I wouldn't give," said she.

"Nothing?" he cried.

"No," said she.

Suddenly, he was standing over her with twitching hands. "I pray to heaven that I don't misunderstand," said he.

"I pray that you don't!" said she.

So, a long time later—it seemed only an instant—the sheriff returned and tapped discreetly on the door.

"It's taken me an hour to get that drink," said he. "May I come in?"

"An hour!" cried the girl.

The door was unlocked. The sheirff stood, with his faint smile, in the doorway.

"A whole hour since he went away?" exclaimed Sherry, and stared at the girl.

But suddenly she smiled, and touched his arm.

"It isn't so very long," said she. "One hour out of a whole life!"

"THE KING OF THE WESTERN NOVEL"
is
MAX BRAND

_____THE BIG TRAIL (75-314, 95¢)
_____THE BLUE JAY (75-468, 95¢)
_____THE BORDER BANDIT (74-218, 75¢)
_____BORDER GUNS (76-315, $1.25)
_____DEAD OR ALIVE (64-708, 75¢)
_____GUNMAN'S LEGACY (74-020, 75¢)
_____THE JACKSON TRAIL (75-540, 95¢)
_____THE KING BIRD RIDES (75-840, 95¢)
_____THE MAN FROM MUSTANG (64-767, 75¢)
_____MOUNTAIN RIDERS (75-932, 95¢)
_____MONTANA RIDES AGAIN (74-418, 75¢)
_____OUTLAW BREED (75-331, 95¢)
_____OUTLAW VALLEY (74-382, 75¢)
_____OUTLAW'S CODE (74-421, 75¢)
_____PILLAR MOUNTAIN (75-486, 95¢)
_____PLEASANT JIM (64-633, 75¢)

 A Warner Communications Company

Please send me the books I have checked.

Enclose check or money order only, no cash please. Plus 25¢ per copy to cover postage and handling. N.Y. State residents add applicable sales tax.

Please allow 2 weeks for delivery.

WARNER BOOKS
P.O. Box 690
New York, N.Y. 10019

Name ....

Address ....

City .... State .... Zip ....

_____ Please send me your free mail order catalog